BRAVE HORSE
The Story of Janus

By

MANLY WADE WELLMAN

ILLUSTRATED BY PETER BURCHARD

COLONIAL WILLIAMSBURG
Williamsburg, Virginia

DISTRIBUTED BY
HOLT, RINEHART AND WINSTON, INC.
New York

A WORLD FAMOUS HORSE STORY LIBRARY Selection

PRINTED IN THE UNITED STATES OF AMERICA

Distributed simultaneously in Canada by
Holt, Rinehart and Winston of Canada, Limited

To the shock troops,
companions on joyous adventures
DOT BARNWELL, FRANK DOBINSON, GAY HOLLAND,
CHERRY PARKER, JUNE STRADER, *and* MENA WEBB

"Each laid hold on each, and each
Found the other strong"
—RUDYARD KIPLING

Contents

BRAVE HORSE

The Story of Janus

I

The Buying of Janus

At Mr. George Grisewood's command, the shabby old groom led a horse out of the broad, stone-fronted stables at El-ford. His chestnut hide gleamed in the June sunlight as Mr. Grisewood's two guests from the American colonies gazed at him.

"There he stands, Janus the son of Janus, and with no weakness save what fate has put upon him," Mr. Grisewood proclaimed.

Young Nick Forrest had listened all through dinner to Grisewood's clipped pronouncements and to Mordecai Booth's drawled observations. The two older men had chatted about His aged Majesty, King George the Second, about what the colonies might hope to do against French arms since Braddock's disaster a year before, and about prices of American tobacco and English cloth. But mostly the talk had concerned the breeding and training of horses to thrill spectators and to win cups and purses at the heroic distance, four galloping miles around a track.

"You seem to prize this nag well, Mr. Grisewood," Mordecai Booth was saying now. "Well indeed, since you invited me all the way to Staffordshire to see and admire him."

Middle age had made Booth sturdy, but not much softer than when he had ridden races in his twenties. His full-skirted coat and snug breeches were of gray cloth, plain woven and well cut. On his bowed, muscular legs he wore glossy boots and on his queued, powdered hair a fine cocked hat. One broad hand tweaked his heavy chin as he gazed at the chestnut horse.

"Aye, and I do prize him," said Grisewood. He was middle-aged, too, but elegantly slender, with snowy ruffles at throat and wrists. His fine coat was dark blue with gold buttons, and his boots had sleek white tops and bore silver spurs at their heels. He offered Booth a jeweled snuffbox, then took a pinch himself, and snapped the lid shut.

"Janus, son of old Janus," said Grisewood again. "His sire was son to the Godolphin Arabian himself. His other blood goes back to the Darley Arabian and the Byerly Turk. He's of racing blood throughout, and the best blood at that."

"And has lived up to it, as I hear," nodded Booth.

"Nobly, sir," Grisewood assured him. "My valued friend Swymmer trained him, and first raced him six years ago, in 1750. I saw him that day. He took the lead in the first mile and never gave it up for the other three, showing his heels to five others, blooded racers all. 'Twas the heroic distance, Mr. Booth, and heroically run."

"Six years ago, you tell us," said Booth. "But now, I hazard, he can scarce walk without limping, much less run."

"Because he strained and fouled the sinew of his near shoulder in 1752. We have a cool June here in Staffordshire, and he shows his lameness. Were it deeper into summer, he'd move less slowly."

"Ha, Nick, what do you think of him?" inquired Booth. "For one thing, he's no tall horse."

Nick Forrest walked close to the chestnut, swiftly estimating the height at the withers. At that point, Janus came not quite to Nick's shoulder, and Nick was a lean young five feet seven. Janus might stand fourteen hands and perhaps a tiny fraction of an inch more.

"No tall horse, Mr. Booth, but no small horse, either," Nick said. "Nothing pony-built about him. He has strong bones and healthy flesh throughout."

Grisewood's fine features relaxed in a grin. "Here's a young cockerel crowing wise," he chuckled. "How old are you, boy?"

"Sixteen last January, but I'll warrant his sense in horse matters," Booth answered for Nick. "His father was long my friend, and rode and judged fine horses as well as any in Virginia. I became Nick's guardian when my old friend died. Nick learned well from his father and adds to his knowledge by daily study."

Nick tried to look modest at that endorsement, but he felt proud.

His godfather Mordecai Booth farmed great tracts of grain and tobacco in Gloucester County, Virginia, and sailed his own vessels across the sea to trade tobacco and bring back goods to his mercantile house in Yorktown. Though he had children of his own, Booth was especially kind to orphans. He had taken Nick to live with him at Belleville plantation and was trustee of the modest legacy from Nick's dead mother and father. Sternly Booth had insisted that Nick learn responsibility and train himself for use in the world and to deserve the name of gentleman.

Nick was dressed much like his guardian, in clothes and boots that were plain but presentable, though he had no powder on his dark hair. In that way and others, Nick tried to be like Mordecai Booth. He considered himself lucky to have been brought on this voyage to England, to have seen ports like Liverpool and fine country estates like Elford, and, just now, to help appraise the worth and character of a horse like this Janus.

As Nick had remarked, Janus was of no great height for a distance racer, but his lines were clean and strong. He carried his large head and curved neck with vigorous grace. Between his brilliant, intelligent eyes showed a white blaze. His right hind foot, too, was white. His back sloped slightly downward from the well-muscled shoulders to speckled hindquarters that looked impressively powerful. And if the legs were a trifle short, their joints were articulated as though for speed. The good length of body, too, might compensate for the shortness of those legs.

"How old is he?" Nick asked the old groom.

"Ten years, young sir."

That was a fairly ripe age for a race horse, Nick told himself, but Janus looked seasoned rather than weakened by years. "Will he suffer me to touch him?"

"Aye, if you're not rough nor sudden."

Nick came closer and ran his hand along the back and neck. There was fine, springy strength under the chestnut hide. Nick drew the mouth open and examined the teeth, healthy for a ten-year-old. Then he moved to Janus' right shoulder and laid his palm there. The skin twitched, the muscles rippled.

"There's where he was hurt," Nick judged aloud.

"That's right, young master," nodded the groom. "Lamed himself winning his last race, he did, poor, brave beast. For a year and more, he could barely hobble."

"But he won, and that proves his pluck," said Grisewood. "Your young Mr. Forrest speaks to Janus' good points, Mr. Booth. If Janus can race no more, he'll yet sire a new generation of fleet sons and daughters to awe your provincial neighbors."

"I was thinking that," said Booth. "What do you reckon a fair price for him?"

"Nay, what say you is a fair price?"

They bargained in friendly fashion, and Nick continued his inspection of Janus. He bent and took the right front hoof in his hands, raised it gently, and felt all the way along the leg up to the seat of injury. Again Janus flinched slightly. Setting the hoof on the ground again, Nick judiciously prodded the flank and slapped the strong, speckled rump.

"He's in full flesh, but not soft," Nick said to the groom. "I take it you exercise him. Can he be ridden?"

"Aye, sir, though never past a walk. Only to stir his feet and his blood, to keep his health."

"And he limps less in midsummer," said Nick thoughtfully. "Why, 'tis near midsummer now. But if he lived where the sun is hotter and brighter, and the air clean and sweet, and the weather mild all year round?"

"I'm thinking he'd thrive there, young master."

Nick gazed into the full, intelligent brown eyes of Janus. He stroked the white-blazed brow, and Janus whinnied softly. Nick smiled at him and walked back to Grisewood and Booth.

"Mr. Booth, you speak wisely and honestly in a true sportsman's spirit, and I vow 'tis pleasure to hear you," Grisewood was saying. "I've found the same good appetite for gentlemanly pursuits in other of you Virginians. There was Colonel Byrd, now. I met him of late, in London."

"Colonel William Byrd of Westover, third of the name," supplied Booth. "He and I are fast friends, and also bitter rivals at hunting and racing and all competitions."

"'Twas said he lost a thousand pounds sterling in a single night at cards with His Grace of Cumberland," went on Grisewood. "Nor did he look woeful at such loss, but paid next morning with a draft written against his London bankers. I remember that I was amazed to hear of an American gentleman with such sums in England, far from home."

"Colonel Byrd has resources and friends both places," said Booth. "But here's Nick with us again, grave and thoughtful."

"If I may say a word about Janus, Mr. Booth," Nick ventured.

"To be sure, lad, a hundred if you like," smiled Booth.

"Here in England, I suspect, the winters are long and cold."

"Tediously long and at times bitter cold," Grisewood assured him. "Seven months of cold weather most years, to make us prize summer the more."

"But in Virginia we have not more than five cold months," Nick pursued, "which leaves us seven warm months, and some of them truly hot."

"Now, Nick, do you think we stand here to be schooled on the weather?" said Booth good-humoredly. "True, our summers are warmer and longer than here in Staffordshire, but what of that?"

Nick gestured toward where the horse stood. "He fares better in warmth than in cold. Had he seven months of it instead of five, and good medicines and good care to boot, who can say, sir? He might run again instead of limping."

Booth knitted his heavy brows. "You repay my kindnesses in poor coin, young Nick. I was arriving at a modest price, to bear Janus home with us. But now your talk will cause Mr. Grisewood to ask me more."

Grisewood laughed merrily.

"I'm no chafferer, Mr. Booth," he said. "I'd never think of selling Janus to you at all, had not our mutual friends praised you in their letters to me. Truth to say, I offer him only because of what young Mr. Forrest says—your warmer Virginia may be a comfort to Janus as he grows older. I'll ask not a penny more than I've said already, and I would never speak to you more cordially were you a born Staffordshireman."

"And I would never hear you more happily were you a born Virginian," replied Booth. "Shall we come to a good agreement then?"

"Back to the house, sir, and we'll draw a bill of sale."

The two gentlemen walked away together, discussing terms. But Nick stayed where he was. Once more he looked at Janus.

"He'll be your horse, young sir," said the old groom.

"Not mine," amended Nick. "It's Mr. Booth who buys him."

"He buys Janus and pays down his money, but Janus will be yours," the groom insisted. "You studied him and saw the hope in him, and it will be you who cares for him and comes to love him well. See, already he looks at you, knowing and friendly. We'll take him back to his stall, and I'll tell you all I know of him and how I've cared for him. Would you like to hear?"

"Gladly," agreed Nick, and his voice sounded truly glad.

II

Mrs. Armistead's Terms

It was nearly fourscore miles from Elford in Staffordshire to Liverpool, where Booth's ship had discharged its freight of tobacco and was taking on a cargo of cloth, farm tools, saddles, casks of wine, bedsteads and tables and chairs, pots and pans and kettles, earthenware, shoes, and a host of goods to be sold through Booth's big trading house at Yorktown in Virginia. On the morning after the purchase of Janus, Booth assigned Nick the responsibility of getting him to Liverpool, while he himself departed by post chaise to supervise the loading of the ship.

He was gone when Nick and the groom led Janus out. Grisewood had provided an old saddle, bridle, and blanket, with pouches to carry necessaries for the journey.

"Godspeed and fair fortune," said Grisewood, taking Nick by the hand. "And to my old friend Janus, better health and better luck in warm Virginia. I count myself fortunate that I could place him in the hands of a colonist like Mr. Booth. I wager there are few like him, or you either, in that wild country."

"It's not so wild, sir," grinned Nick. "We don't live in wigwams, nor must we fight Indians daily. I honor Mr. Booth as my guardian and friend, but we have good Virginia neighbors, who'll give Janus a friendly welcome."

"Ride him slow and easy at first," advised the groom. "An hour on the way and he'll be moving less stiffly."

7

"Nay, he and I shall walk that first hour together," said Nick, the reins in his hand. "That way, we'll both limber ourselves and become better company for each other. Nor shall I forget your advice about hot cloths on his shoulder night and morning. My thanks to you both for hospitality and friendship."

They took the highway leading west. Janus favored his right foreleg at first, but slow, steady walking brought him to more assurance and, Nick hoped, an easing of the stiffness. Nick judged time by the sun's motion and reckoned that in an hour's trudging they had covered some three miles. He then mounted Janus, riding at an easy walk.

"I am glad, Janus, that I ride at no more than a hundred and twenty pounds," said Nick. "I'll keep an easy rein, and force you to no speed whatever."

Janus uttered his soft whinny, and Nick patted his neck. "Good horse. You understand my speech, and I begin to understand yours."

Later that morning, Nick dismounted to let Janus rest and crop grass at the roadside. Then both walked on for another hour. At noon, Nick ate bread and cheese in the yard of a country inn while a hostler rubbed Janus down. They both had supper at an inn in a village and went on in the bright summer evening, until Nick dismounted at twilight at yet another hostelry. He himself curried Janus and dipped a cloth in hot water to drape on the sore shoulder. They had gone slowly, with frequent rests, but the long day had seen them travel perhaps twenty-five miles.

In that fashion they covered the distance to Liverpool in three days. At dark of the third day, Mordecai Booth welcomed them at his water-front tavern. Janus showed no great weariness from the ordeal as they saw him into the care of the stableman. Then Nick sat down with Booth to a late supper in the dining room.

"You made good time, youngster, and our Janus seems to have thrived," said Booth as he helped Nick to pigeon pie. "I gave you a great responsibility, and you've deserved my trust."

"Indeed he went pluckily," said Nick. "Each night I put cloths to his shoulder, as hot as he could stand, and when he was eased I rubbed the place well. I know you set great store by him."

"In sooth, I do," vowed Booth, sipping wine. "There's brave

blood to Janus, as he proved on the track when he was young and sound. He'll sire us swift colts in Virginia."

"You count on him as the sire of winners?"

"Why else fetch him home?" demanded Booth. "Ha, Nick, you'll see covetous eyes in the faces of our friends—Ralph Wormeley, William Nelson, John Tayloe. Even Colonel Byrd, who swears that his new-imported Valiant will outshine his other four-mile racer, Tryall."

Valiant had better run faster than Tryall, Nick reflected. He remembered a meeting at the Gloucester race ground four years earlier, when four Virginia horses were beaten at four miles, twice around the track, by Selima, Colonel Tasker's swift bay mare from Maryland. Tryall had run only second best that day, and Byrd had mourned.

William Byrd III was a proud, heavy-faced patrician among planters, a leader in politics and society, and a passionate gambler to boot. If he had lost a thousand pounds in one night at cards, as Grisewood had said, he had won similar great sums at other gaming ventures. He was colonel of a Virginia militia regiment, which he equipped and paid from his own considerable funds. And he believed himself the wisest and surest of racing men on all the American turf. With his new bay horse Valiant, tall, beautiful, and swift, he frankly proposed to drive all rivals from the race tracks, wherever any beast could be found to challenge him.

"Valiant's time will be short," predicted Booth, passing Nick the cheese. "We'll find mares worthy to mate with Janus. Five years hence, with a fleet four-year-old colt—"

He broke off, half wistfully.

"Could Janus but race again," Nick ventured.

"Nay, his racing days are past," Booth said. "We must wait for his children to run as once he ran."

"I'll try to cure his crippling hurts," Nick insisted.

"Try, then," granted Booth. "But there are other matters now on my mind."

He went on to tell Nick frankly that his plantations did not bring him enough money to do the things he most enjoyed. He spoke of trade with England, the selling of tobacco and the buying of manufactured goods on which to build prosperity in Virginia. He was unhappy because his lands were heavily encumbered with debt, and he spoke hopefully of paying his obligations through this latest trading expedition. Then he spoke of his greatest interest, owning and training and racing splendid horses.

"I grow old, Nick, but my joy in swift racing stays young," he declared. "You love horses, too, and you understand my feeling."

Several days were spent in completing the cargo. On the final morning, Nick led Janus to the wharf where the vessel was moored. Workmen rigged a folded canvas under Janus' belly and hooked it to a tackle, which lifted Janus bodily to the deck. Nick hurried aboard to set him free and lead him carefully down sloping planks to where a stall had been prepared in the hold. As they sailed with the tide, Nick stood with Janus.

"I'll be with you every day," Nick comforted him. "In Virginia you'll find yourself anew, with four good legs under you instead of three."

Nearly four weeks it took them to reach the mouth of the York River. At noon on a hot, bright July day, they entered the broad stream and trimmed sail to put in toward the southern shore, where among surrounding green forests lay Yorktown. Great craft and small rode at anchor or were tied up close to the wharves. Carefully the ship worked her way to the outer end of a long dock. The sailors flung lines ashore to waiting hands that drew her close and made her fast.

Mordecai Booth was first down the gangplank, issuing orders to a throng of workmen. Nick led Janus up a ramp to the deck, then down the plank.

"You're stiff from no exercise," Nick said. "Set your hoofs to these cleats. And look about you, Janus. Here's Virginia, and before many hours we'll be across river and up to Belleville."

He led Janus shoreward, past stout Negro workmen with barrows and carts to unload the cargo. Water-front loafers stared curiously as Nick halted Janus beside Booth's warehouse, on hard earth.

Across the river-front street stood a public house. Excited voices rose at its open door, where two men in military uniform stood and argued. One wore the red coat and gold-laced hat of a British officer, with white stockings and buckled shoes. His dark hair was smartly clubbed, and his flushed face was almost as red as his coat. He was tall, but his companion towered above him.

This giant of a man was dressed in the dark-blue coat of an officer of Virginia volunteers, with scarlet facings at collar, cuffs, and pocket flaps. The heavy epaulettes of a colonel rode his wide shoulders. A straight sword hung at his side, and his white breeches and black boots were snug to long, powerful legs. His hair was brown, and his face looked vigorously ruddy. It was set with a great blade of a nose. He spoke in a voice that carried to where Nick stood with Janus.

"You shall not go yonder to that house, Captain Magworth," boomed out the big colonel. "I've ridden swift from Williamsburg, where Governor Dinwiddie and his staff know how you cheated at your accounts and falsified the books. If you don't resign, and that swiftly, you'll be court-martialed and publicly disgraced."

"I'll stand no insolence from you, Colonel Washington," protested the other, his own voice rising. "I hold the king's commission, and I am an English gentleman of reputation—"

"Of your reputation in England I know nothing," broke in the colonel, "but here in Virginia it's a sorry one. Begone, sir, and never let me see your face again, in or out of service."

The man gestured, in appeal or menace, or both. Then he fairly darted into the public house. The colonel relaxed and glanced across at Nick. At once he came striding.

"Here's a horse that I don't know, and at first sight a fine bit of blood," he said. "How is he called, young sir?"

"Janus is his name, and he is just landed from a voyage from England," replied Nick. "He belongs to Mr. Mordecai Booth of Belleville."

"Aye, I have the honor of Mr. Booth's acquaintance."

"And I know who you are, sir," Nick decided to say. "Colonel Washington, of the First Virginia Regiment. I am Nick Forrest."

Washington smiled slightly. His height and his strong features made him look older than his twenty-four years. Like Nick, most Virginians knew him for his bold and soldierly record, particularly in saving the remains of Braddock's defeated army in 1755.

"I knew a Mr. Nicholas Forrest of Gloucester County, years back when I was perhaps your age," Washington said.

"He was my father, Colonel Washington."

"He was captain of militia when I was not yet commissioned. If you are like your father in any way, count me your friend as he counted me his." Washington surveyed Janus with expert eyes. "This horse has the look of speed and strength and great endurance."

"If only he weren't lame, sir," said Nick. "Years ago he strained and fouled a shoulder sinew. It's my hope I can help him heal."

He found himself talking readily to this sympathetic new friend, of his theory that warmer weather, careful treatment, and good medicine could help Janus. Washington spoke encouragingly, telling his own experience in treating lame horses. The two discussed fomentations of turpentine, mustard water, and other mixtures as though they had been old acquaintances. Nick did not at first see Mordecai Booth strolling close to listen.

"Mr. Booth, welcome home," Washington said. "I've been looking at your new stallion and making the acquaintance of Mr. Forrest, whom I find to be the son of an old friend like yourself."

"Your servant, Colonel Washington," rejoined Booth. "How go our military affairs, and what brings you to Yorktown?"

"A melancholy errand," said Washington. "His Excellency Governor Dinwiddie attached a visiting British officer to our staff, and we trusted him for purchase of supplies and record of pay to the troops. But public funds found their way into his pockets, and I came here as he was seeking to steal even more. Just now I spoke roundly to him and let him know that the service will thrive better without his help."

Another figure came toward them. It was a woman, and a very impressive woman indeed. For all her evident age, she carried her small, plump self with proud vigor. Her abundant, high-piled hair needed no powder to make it white as thistledown. Her summer dress of figured India cotton was elaborately flounced and panniered. One hand bore a bright blue parasol to fend off the sun, the other a net purse sewn with beads. Her features were finely chiseled, and her expression as commanding as Washington's. Behind her walked a spruce brown man in neat footman's apparel, his arms loaded with parcels as though from a shopping expedition. Nick knew her well and liked her, although he stood in awe of her.

"Mistress Armistead," he said as she came near, and Booth and Washington doffed their hats and bowed as one.

"You're home again, son-in-law," she greeted Booth. "Colonel Washington, I rejoice to see you. And Nick, too. Who's this stranger?" She flourished her purse at Janus.

"A fine purchase from England, ma'am," answered Booth. "Janus is his name, and he's grandson to the renowned Godolphin Arabian."

Mrs. Armistead looked Janus over from nose to tail as expertly as had Washington.

"Will he outrun Colonel Byrd's Valiant?" she demanded.

"No, because—," Booth began.

"I dare hope—," said Nick at the same moment.

Washington said courteous farewells and strode away. Mrs. Armistead looked with bright black eyes from Booth to Nick, then back again.

"Which is right?" she prodded them. "Will he run or not? Come, I'm past three score and ten and too old to wait tedious times for answers to my questions."

Nick dutifully told the story of Janus: how he had raced victoriously in his youth and had lamed himself racing; how he had stayed lame in the English climate; and how, with care and good fortune, he might be brought to racing form again. Mrs. Armistead listened, with the stern attention of a judge hearing evidence in court.

"The voyage was profitable all around," said Booth. "I hope to be able to pay the debts of my plantation. I left you here with my power of attorney in the matter, ma'am. Do my creditors press hard?"

"Your debts are paid," said Mrs. Armistead, fixing her brilliant eyes on Booth.

"How is that possible?" he asked her.

"While you've been abroad, your creditors urged their accounts for prompt payment. As your representative, I received notice that your Belleville house and lands would be sold for the amount of the money you owed. The sale by Sheriff Randolph was accomplished in May."

She spoke casually, almost cheerfully, but Booth's sturdy form seemed to totter.

"Alack, and I abroad!" he cried. "Am I then without a home, without shelter, like any vagabond?"

Mrs. Armistead did not seem to hear him. She studied Janus again.

"He has the look of a high-mettled horse," she observed. "And you think to heal him, Nick? If you can, there may have been good in you and Mr. Booth gallivanting abroad."

"Who bought Belleville?" Booth stammered out.

"I did, Mordecai," Mrs. Armistead half purred. "I was at the sale and bought in your properties, at the figure of your debts."

Booth breathed deeply, and his pale, set face relaxed a trifle.

"Then they'll be mine again," he said, "as soon as I pay you—"

"Not so fast," she bade him. "You're no success as a planter. And if I gave Belleville to my daughter, she'd turn it all over to you. My lawyers are drawing an agreement between Anna Armistead on one hand and Mordecai and Joyce Booth on the other."

"Am I to have my home again?" Booth pleaded. "Speak, I entreat you."

"You shall have it, but only in deed of trust," pronounced Mrs. Armistead. "The property will revert to your son, George—he, at least, knows the planting life and the planting labor. He can make the land profitable, perhaps."

Booth seemed to recover some of his poise. "Zounds, ma'am, that's generous indeed," he said gratefully. "When shall we sign?"

But Mrs. Armistead was walking around Janus. She looked into his eyes, into his fine, flaring nostrils. She put her wise old hand on his cheek.

"There's another condition, Mordecai," she announced at last. "You, too, Nick, give me your attention. I'm tired of hearing Colonel William Byrd's talk of how his Valiant won the spring races, both yonder at Williamsburg and up at our Gloucester course. Mend this limping Janus to beat him and stop his boasts. Then I'm well repaid of my time and money, and the conveyance shall be made." She surveyed them both in turn. "Is it agreed?"

"Agreed," said Booth desperately and Nick happily, as if in the same breath.

III

Home to Belleville

Booth made businesslike haste to arrange the movement of his trade goods to his storehouse and left details with a trusted subordinate. At his dock was moored a light, swift, sloop, easily handled in the tributaries of the York, and he invited his mother-in-law to join him in his homeward sail to Belleville. There, said Booth, he would be happy to have her company at dinner, and later a carriage would take her to her own house nearby. But she chose to be a passenger on the bigger, heavier barge, aboard which Nick was leading Janus.

"If the family interests are somewhat bound up in that horse, I mean to know more about him," she said. "No time like the present."

One Negro servant took the tiller, and another stood ready to handle the sails. Mrs. Armistead sat on a crate of crockery, her parasol on high, and the footman piled her packages beside her. As the barge made its ponderous way across the York and east of Gloucester Point toward Ware Neck on North River, she talked to both Nick and Janus. Nick answered a hundred questions as best he could.

"You did well to hear Colonel Washington," she commented, "for he's as knowing with horses as with soldiers. His suggestion of mustard water is sound. But be cautious with such strong application, Nick. Enough will help, but too much will blister."

17

Janus seemed to know he was the subject of conversation and watched them with every appearance of courteous interest.

"I'll visit you to see how Janus fares," Mrs. Armistead went on, "and bring along a new friend for you. She's a young cousin of mine, Nancy Tyll. When her parents died last winter I took her into my home, as Mr. Booth took you into his."

"I will be honored to meet any connection of yours, ma'am," said Nick promptly.

"La, there speaks the born gentleman. Young Nancy has manners, too, and good school learning from the tutor I found for her. But she's lacking in some matters every well-bred girl should know. Horses, for one. Mayhap you can mend her ignorance there."

By late afternoon the barge moved toward the western shore of North River, to where tall, shady trees stood around the great plantation house of Belleville. Booth's sailboat was already tied up to the small dock. The barge docked, and Nick led Janus ashore and up the broad driveway toward the home of the Booths.

It was a large, gabled building, both, solid and graceful of design. Steps mounted to its broad front door. Mostly the house was of wood, but one wing dating back a full century was of white-painted brick. Down the steps came Booth, to welcome his mother-in-law and to speak to Nick.

"To the stables with Janus, and introduce him to Saul," Booth directed Nick. "Then you'll want to change clothes and come to the house." To Mrs. Armistead he said, "Your ward Nancy waits here for you. She plays the spinet most tunefully."

"Egad, she'd better, or the money for her lessons is wasted," said Mrs. Armistead. "Hark, I hear her playing now."

Melodious, hushed music drifted through a window.

"A minuet," Mrs. Armistead murmured. "It could make me forget my years and crotchets and tread a measure. Would we'd brought Colonel Washington with us, he's a fine dancer."

Nick urged Janus around the house to the right, past the old brick wing where he kept his own living quarters. Behind were a garden for flowers and another for fresh vegetables, with a shady rose-covered pavilion and small buildings for tools and storage. They went along a path to a timber-fronted structure, almost as long as the big house, which contained the carriage sheds and the stables.

Someone waited there, a dignified man in a broad hat and linen vest. He had a wise, brown face and powerful, stooped shoulders. When he saw Nick and Janus, he swung wide the gate of the railed paddock.

"Saul," Nick hailed him. "'Tis glad I am to be home."

"And glad I am to say welcome, Master Nick," returned Saul, his white teeth flashing a smile. "Master Booth said that this horse is called Janus."

Nick brought Janus into the paddock. Saul walked all the way around Janus, surveying every point with knowing interest. Middle-aged, intelligent, deeply versed in all aspects of horse lore, Saul was Booth's most prized and respected servant. He and Nick were fast friends. And another friend was Saul's son Scipio, a good rider and exerciser of horses, who came out of the stables to join them.

Scipio was in his twenties, taller than Saul and leaner, dressed in riding breeches and old boots.

Saul's wise hand stroked Janus' right shoulder as Nick told of the injured sinew that had so long been giving trouble.

"We'll start this night to make him feel better," Saul promised. "A hot poultice, and a warm blanket for him when the sun goes down and the air cools."

"And tomorrow early we'll take further counsel upon him," said Nick. "Just now I'm wanted at the big house."

But even as he spoke he saw people approaching the paddock gate. Mordecai Booth was one of them, and holding to his arm came Mrs. Joyce Booth, his pleasant-faced, honey-haired wife. Anna Armistead hurried along at Booth's other side. Behind the Booths two others walked side by side, tall, handsome Colonel John Tayloe of Mount Airy on the Rappahannock and a girl whom Nick did not recognize.

"We're come to look at Janus," called out Booth. "'Twas at Mrs. Armistead's insistence."

"Aye, for he is fit company for the best," was Mrs. Armistead's ringing declaration. "Indeed, I prefer most horses to most men and women. They are handsome creatures, they are true to trust and prompt to duty, and they seldom if ever interrupt me when I am talking."

John Tayloe lifted a hand in greeting to Nick. He was a fine-featured, faultlessly dressed gentleman in his thirties. Virginia society admired him. He was one of the region's most expert and devoted racers of horses, and he had a reputation for gambling almost as great as that of William Byrd's.

"Nick, suffer me to present you to my young cousin Nancy Tyll," Mrs. Armistead was saying. "Nancy, I spoke but now about Nick Forrest. Be acquainted, you two, whilst we give our attention to Janus."

Nick whipped off his hat and faced Nancy Tyll. She was about his own age, he guessed, and she was slim but vigorous of figure and as tall as himself. Her features were handsomely bold, and her fine, dark hair abundant. She returned Nick's gaze with luminous eyes like dark green opals. For the first time that day, Nick took time to think how he was dressed.

He had come from the ship in the rumpled suit he had worn for most of the voyage. He had pulled off the coat and carried it over his lean forearm, and his shirt sleeves were rolled up. He knew that his hair was tousled by wind on the journey home in the barge, and very probably his face was smudged. He ventured a bow, nothing so assured as the bows of Mordecai Booth or George Washington.

"Yours to command, Miss Tyll," he said, as gravely as his sixteen years could manage. "I trust that you find the day pleasant and that you, too, like horses."

"I like them well enough," she returned, in a soft voice that seemed to muster its own show of dignity. "Yet I know nothing witty or helpful to say of them."

She moved two or three steps away from the group, her full, flounced yellow skirt swaying. Nick thought that her height gave her stateliness, and wished he knew whether she thought him untidy and stable-bred.

"Come here, Nick," Mrs. Armistead summoned him imperiously. "Let's hear again your opinion on Janus and how he may run yet."

Nick obeyed her gladly, for just then Nancy Tyll awed him more than did Mrs. Armistead. Coming to where Saul held Janus by the halter, he told his oft-rehearsed story of how Janus had raced, how he had gone lame, and how possibly he might recover.

"See to his right shoulder here," Nick invited, spreading his hand upon it. "He winces. But the muscle is not shrunk away, as 'twould be if he had no strength or motion left."

"Amen to that wise young word," applauded Mrs. Armistead. "I agree with Nick in these thoughts, Colonel Tayloe."

"You may be right, ma'am," said the master of Mount Airy. "Yet I'd lief see him with longer legs to run swiftly."

"His stride may not be long, Colonel Tayloe," suggested Nick, "but in good health he might move faster by swifter motion."

"Even so, even so," endorsed Mrs. Armistead. "I can see him taking two steps to one of a long-legged beast. You, Colonel Tayloe, once set great store by the striding action of your stallion Childers. Yet remember the Gloucester race meet in 1752, when Colonel Tasker's Selima won and distanced your Childers by a furlong."

"I'm not likely to forget it, ma'am," confessed Tayloe dolefully. "I lost five hundred pistoles in gold to Tasker that day, and another five hundred to Colonel Byrd, whose Tryall came in second."

"We'll see Janus a winner and a champion," Mrs. Armistead cried confidently. "The thought makes me feel as young as Nancy Tyll."

In her high spirits she slapped Janus on the haunch so smartly that he started and nearly sprang forward.

Nancy Tyll had been listening, with a mute politeness that seemed to partake of boredom. Nick told himself that her clear-cut features might well turn lofty and severe. When Saul led Janus away and the party turned toward the house, Colonel Tayloe escorted Mrs. Armistead. Booth followed them with his lady. Nick walked with Nancy only because he seemed told to do so.

"You're vastly knowledgeable about horses, Mr. Forrest," she said, again as though she were politely bored.

"I strive to inform myself, Miss Tyll," he ventured, himself growing heavy-mannered. "To learn other things too, for an honest place and honest use in the world." He looked at her sidelong. "I heard you playing the spinet in yonder."

"I'm no skilled performer," she said, "and my taste lies in other fields."

"Indeed, ma'am?"

"I school myself, as you say you do, for usefulness," said she, measuring out her words. "Though perhaps I'll never find usefulness worth my labor and planning." She threw back her head, and her firm round chin came forward. "The world dully refuses to let women be of true worth or consequence."

"How, ma'am!" cried Nick in amazement. "Sure, women are of the utmost consequence, in the home, in society—"

"Aye, with men strutting and bowing and paying court, if so be a woman is pretty," she interrupted him. "Turning pages of music for them to play, craving their company in the dance, making silly compliments to flatter. But otherwise, what can a woman hope to do for the public good? Can she sit in the House of Burgesses at Williamsburg? Would any person give a moment's thought to a wise, able woman as governor?"

Nick only stared. He had never heard such a suggestion in his life.

"No, never," she answered her own question. "Let her play sprightly music, let her tread a dance measure, take a cup of tea brought by some mincing gallant, smile at his empty compliments. Other times, she may embroider kerchiefs, or weigh out provisions for servants, or cull garden flowers. Even your horses are better respected, and far better valued if they can run a swift four miles and win purses and prizes and wagers."

They were beside the house now, and Nick was heartily glad. Not Mrs. Armistead herself had ever so daunted him.

"We look for you at table in good time, Nick," said Booth over his shoulder.

"I'll hasten to make myself presentable, sir," Nick said, and turned to enter the door of the old wing.

Up a flight of stairs he trotted to his room above. The servants had fetched in his luggage, and he opened a trunk to search out a fresh frilled shirt. Then he stripped to the waist and worried off his dusty boots. At the washstand, he filled a china basin from a pitcher, took a bar of soap, and scrubbed himself well.

He surveyed himself in the glass. He was clean again, but no impressively handsome sight even so. His young face had a long chin and lean lips, with the cheeks flat and the dark eyes set deep. He frowned at himself as he searched out a razor that had been his father's, rubbed sudsy lather on his jaws, and shaved away some downy stubble. Finally he combed his black hair and tied it at the nape of his neck with a silk ribbon.

He drew on the frilled shirt and sought out what he considered his finest suit, blue striped silk coat and breeches, with covered buttons. He chose a wine-colored vest. He slid his young shanks into white stockings and put on low, broad-heeled black shoes with silver buckles. Again he gazed at his reflection in the mirror and frowned as before, but this time in something of somber approval. He spread the fingers of his right hand upon the vest and bowed ceremoniously to himself.

Out he went and downstairs and around to the great front door. At least he looked like a gentleman now, and so Mrs. Armistead's ward Nancy Tyll must recognize, however she seemed to think that knowledge of horses was no respectable knowledge at all.

IV

"Lame No More"

The sun was up early next morning, but not as early as Nick. On the way to the stables in the first gray light, he thought of dinner the previous evening, the cheerful talk of Mr. and Mrs. Booth, the emphatic declarations of Mrs. Armistead, and the urbanity of Colonel Tayloe. He thought too, of Nancy Tyll's highly serious and highly infrequent remarks, and of how, when he had watched the light carriage take her and Mrs. Armistead away home, she had not looked back at all.

Saul was rubbing Janus' legs with a hot cloth, and Scipio sat on an upturned bucket, twisting brown, crackly strips together.

"Corn blades or shucks?" asked Nick.

"Blades from the stalks, Master Nick," said Scipio. "Shucks off the ears don't nourish well. These come from last fall's cutting. We'll have fresh-dried blades when we take the early crop, end of the month."

Beside Scipio were stacked other twists of dry blades, like billets of kindling. Nick stooped for one and nodded satisfaction. That was the best fodder for horses, under any conditioning program.

"His feed's ready, too," added Saul. "Oats hulled and winnowed, corn chopped coarse and washed to float off the husk and chaff. You could make that corn into porridge for folks."

"You're several laps ahead of me," Nick laughed, and looked eastward at the sun peeping over the treetops. "Suppose I walk him four miles before he eats."

"Shall I saddle him?" Saul offered.

24

"Better for him to walk light. Put his blanket back on, and I'll ride Penny." And Nick pointed to another stall, where a little dun mare blinked drowsily.

He rode out at a side gate of the paddock, keeping Penny reined to a walk and on his left leading the blanket-draped Janus by a long halter rope. They took a path that led among green groves and fields of corn, peas, and tobacco behind Belleville. Here and there, gangs of field hands in coarse shirts and breeches plied their hoes under the eyes of overseers. The path led up a gentle slope, and Nick observed that Janus dragged the toe of his right hoof, sure mark of a shoulder strain. But the drag was not heavy or clumsy.

When they returned, Saul waited to give Janus another rubdown. Stripping off the blanket, he used a sweat knife, made of an old broken sword with the edge dulled, to clear away the perspiration, as a barber shaves off lather. Then he rubbed and curried Janus all over. For the ailing shoulder he used two cloths, one soaking in a pail of hot water while he rubbed with the other.

Finally, Janus was allowed to eat grain and twisted blades, but not too much, and Saul gave him water.

"Forty swallows," cautioned Nick. "No more and no less."

"That's for training a horse before a race," said Scipio.

"I want to train him somewhat in that fashion," Nick told them. "Only slowly and carefully."

After eating, Janus, under a blanket, was turned into a smaller enclosure next to the main paddock. At midafternoon, Nick again rode out on Penny, leading Janus on the four-mile way. The ride was followed by the same ration of hulled oats, cracked corn, and forty swallows of water.

There were seven more days of similar cautious exercise. Twice, Booth rode along on his favorite sorrel hunter, Dragoon. Feed and water, too, were carefully supervised, and a series of hot poultices was applied to Janus' shoulder.

Mrs. Armistead came to oversee one such preparation. She brought a flask of white vitriol, which she herself had made of zinc and sulphuric acid, and called for sugar of lead from the stable medicine cabinet. At her orders, Scipio boiled a strong infusion of the inner bark of the elm. Into a measure of this, Mrs. Armistead mixed the other ingredients.

"Set it to his shoulder, as hot as he can stand," she said.

Saul did so, but alternated this strong fomentation with one of his own concoction. Rue and bay leaves went into it, and it made the stable smell like a kitchen.

"It's the heat helps most," he said to Nick, out of Mrs. Armistead's hearing. "We mustn't blister him, just make the blood run fast."

When the eight days were done, Nick came out on the ninth morning to see Janus standing with something of firmness. His right front hoof was set flat instead of tilting to rest on its toe. Scipio pointed out this favorable sign.

"He does famously," said Scipio. "Shall I ride him, Master Nick?"

"You ride twenty pounds heavier than I do," Nick replied. "Saddle him for me, I'll take him a two-mile walk, and you come along on Penny. We'll both watch his action."

They set out along a plantation path. Nick kept Janus to a walk,

but it seemed that Janus did not check so easily as when they had traveled from Staffordshire to Liverpool in June. From time to time, Nick put his right hand forward to feel the shoulder. The muscles slid and bunched in a way that made Nick hope that there was no serious misplacement of the damaged tendon.

"See, he wants to race with Penny here," said Scipio, leaning to study Janus.

"That will come later," said Nick. "Slow mending is sure mending. Does he drag with his right front foot?"

"A trifle," Scipio reported.

Janus seemed to improve with every day. Nick and Saul credited the hot weather for much of this. They kept Janus clad in a blanket each night, and continued with poultice applications to the right shoulder. A third eight-day period came to an end. As August followed July, they rejoiced at how Janus responded to exercise and treatment.

Booth, too, was pleased to hear of this progress. "All this is vastly well," he said at the dinner table. "Yet, Nick, there are other things than horse-healing." He looked across at his son George. "And other than crop-growing, my son."

"Father, I predict a rich harvest for Belleville this year—tobacco, hemp, and grain," said young George earnestly. "'Tis time that Virginia land became worth a planter's labor and study. Good crops at good prices will help our affairs, along with your trade at York-town and overseas in England."

"'Tis for that reason I urge you back to reading botany and husbandry and account-keeping," said his father. "As for you, Nick, how goes your Latin and arithmetic? These are as important to a gentleman's education as ever are horses."

Nancy Tyll would have seconded that view, Nick thought. But he said only, "I read and study each night, sir. I hope 'tis to my benefit."

On the first morning of the next eight days, Nick came out, early as usual. He smiled as Saul led Janus out, saddled and bridled.

"Make ready his breakfast, and I'll exercise him in close reach of it," said Nick. "On the exercise track yonder."

He mounted Janus and rode toward the half-mile oval behind the stables, where Mordecai Booth trained racers and young saddle horses. Scipio sat on a rail to watch as Nick put Janus to the track, in a brisk walk.

He did not check Janus so resolutely. Janus moved readily and eagerly for a hundred yards and then, when Nick slacked the rein, quickened his ambling pace. He moved nimbly, surely, and easily, all the way to the track's far curve. Then Nick slowed him to a walk and brought him back to where Scipio waited.

"I watched," called Scipio. "All four feet moved sure and strong."

"We'll go round again," said Nick.

He started Janus a second time, with even less pull on the reins. Janus increased his pace, almost to a canter. Nick rode leaning forward, his right hand on the shoulder. Halfway around the track they went. Then Nick pulled Janus to a walk for a few yards, feeling the shoulder's motion and listening intently to how Janus breathed and how his feet sounded as they struck the earth. Satisfied, he let Janus canter, all the way back to Scipio.

Twice more around they went, alternately walking and cantering, before Nick brought Janus back to the paddock. Plainly Janus had not overworked to achieve that brisk gait, and in the afternoon Nick tried him again, faster and for longer stretches.

There was company at Belleville the next day. Colonel William Byrd visited Mordecai Booth. He came with Booth to watch Janus run on the track in the afternoon. Byrd was a full-fed, droopy-lidded man in his early forties, with flushed cheeks and black hair. Leaning on a gold-headed cane, he watched Janus run and walk alternately. For one stretch, Nick let Janus quicken his pace almost to a full gallop.

"Zounds, Mr. Booth," said Byrd when Nick dismounted, "is this the beast you brought in such high hopes from England?" He regarded Janus from under heavy lids. "Sure, he's no figure of a horse for our Virginia tracks."

"He did well in England when he was young," reminded Booth.

"Aye, but he's a ripe ten years old and has the extra flesh for a dignified age," drawled Byrd. "And I do not admire his action. He scampers and scurries, like a frightened field mouse.

"'Twas his first running in a long time," said Nick, loosening the girth. "He'll do better with each passing day."

"Maybe," granted Byrd, as though he doubted it. "Mr. Booth, once you raced many horses, but now you have only this one half-crippled nag. I'm distressed you have nothing better to train against good blooded horses. My own Valiant, for example."

"Give me and Janus time, and we may challenge that Valiant of yours," said Booth, a trifle nettled.

"Whenever it so pleases you."

The two walked away, and Nick led Janus back to the stables.

Each day for four days, Nick worked Janus on the track for two miles, mornings and evenings. By the fourth day, Janus was running a half-mile at a time, and not once as though he wanted to stop.

The fifth day was Saturday, August 7. Mrs. Armistead came visiting, and with her was Nancy Tyll. At dinner, Mrs. Armistead asked her usual many questions about Janus.

"I've tended him these twenty-nine days," Nick calculated. "And I rejoice to say that he is lame no more."

"Lame no more!" cried Mrs. Armistead. "Come, it sounds well in all our ears."

"I intend to take him four or five miles this afternoon, ma'am," said Nick. "Running and jogging."

"Then Nancy shall ride with you," decreed Mrs. Armistead. "'Twill do the child good, I vow."

"I have no riding things," Nancy demurred from where she sat opposite Nick.

"Nay, you may borrow mine," offered Mrs. Booth. "We're not too far from the same size."

"All the same—," Nancy began.

"'Tis not all the same, young miss," Mrs. Armistead swept aside the words. "You get too little fresh air. Do my bidding, and no more bridlings and debatings."

"And I'll ride with you, too," volunteered Mordecai Booth.

Nancy went with Mrs. Booth to don riding clothes, while Booth and Nick went to the stables to order Janus, Dragoon, and Penny saddled. Nancy came to join them, in a brown habit that might better have suited Mrs. Booth's rosy blondeness than Nancy's dark hair and olive skin. The brim of her round hat was caught up in front with a silver buckle, and she carried a riding switch in her gloved hand.

Nick held out his hand, but Nancy did not touch it. Unaided, she set her booted foot to the stirrup and mounted Penny. The three rode together, out to the public road.

Janus wanted to canter, but Nick held him for a mile's walk first, then let him run. Booth on Dragoon and Nancy on Penny followed. When Nick reined Janus to a a slower gait and looked back, he saw the sorrel and the dun loping side by side. Nancy seemed well in control of her mount, and Nick said so as she came close.

"If I am not versed in horse care, yet I have learned something of riding," she said. "Indeed, riding is necessary."

"True, young miss," said Mordecai Booth. "I've known Virginians to tramp five miles to catch a horse, in order to ride him two. And we've ridden two miles, and yonder is something of interest."

They had come out upon the road to Gloucester Court House,

and it was busy with horses and people. A crossroads tavern stood there, plainly doing brisk business. Behind it spread a throng of men and women, black and white, for hundreds of yards.

"A quarter race," Booth exclaimed. "I'd forgotten this was the day. Three good nags, for a purse of ten pistoles—let's watch."

He rode into a lane that led behind the eager watchers. Rising in his stirrups, Nick saw where the contending riders led their horses to the starting point. Booth led the way to the far end of the quarter-mile path. There stood two posts, with red streamers at their tops. Booth pointed to show where a line had been scratched in the ground from post to post, for the finish.

"We're just in time," said Booth. "Even now they mount."

Someone yelled for spectators to draw back from the track. The three riders vaulted into their saddles, and the horses drew up side by side. Dead silence, then the distant flat tap of a drum. A sky-rending chorus of yells as the racers sprang away.

Toward the finish they came, three scampering brown horses, with the riders plying whips. Almost at the first moment, the horse on the left was ahead. Then the center horse drew alongside and came to the front by the length of his outthrust nose. Nearer they came, larger each moment to the eye. A great final cheer as the center horse flashed between the post a winner. The one at the left finished almost at his shoulder, the third a length behind.

There were babbles of talk, exultation here, disappointment there. Nick saw a flash of silver—a bet was being paid. A man in fine tan riding coat and breeches had dismounted from his own horse and was accepting money from several companions.

"A short race," Nancy commented.

"But well run," said Booth, "and none of the three faltered. Though I prefer the distance race by blooded horses, I won't turn from watching a good quarter run. Such quarter-racing has been Virginia's pleasure these hundred years."

"I didn't like to see the horses whipped to that speed," Nancy murmured.

"Nor did I," agreed Booth. "My admiration is for a horse who'll run his mighty best without touch of whip or spur. But Nick says nothing. Did you not like the race?"

Nick watched the elegant man who was taking money from the others. Tall, red-faced, the fellow laughed over his gains.

"I liked it well enough, sir," said Nick to Booth. "I but wondered where I'd seen that gentleman before today."

Booth looked, too. "Nay, he's strange to me. But he chose the winner just now. Will you speak to him, Nick?"

"Not I," and Nick shook his head. "I can't remember him, I say, but I connect him in my mind with some unpleasantness."

V

Four Horses, Four Miles

Mordecai Booth's sober insistence on studies and Nancy Tyll's cool attitude toward horse wisdom had their effect on Nick. Each night he lighted his candle and pored over books. He strove to teach himself to keep accounts, to read Latin verse, and to relish the wit and wisdom of Francis Bacon, Jonathan Swift, and others. But every morning at sunrise and most of every day until sunset, he was with Janus.

Janus gained vigor and assurance with each run. They turned him out of the railed yard into a meadow. He grazed and trotted and loped happily. He grew hard to catch, too, if Saul or Scipio came near with a halter. But Nick need only call his name for him to approach at once.

Penny could not keep up with Janus on the track or along the paths. One morning at breakfast, Nick sought Booth's permission to use the sorrel Dragoon as a running companion for Janus.

"Aye, 'twill be good for both animals," Booth granted the request. "Dragoon was sired by Colonel Byrd's Tryall, and his dam, you'll remember, was a saddle mare of good wind and action. Dragoon strides away famously, and his endurance is considerable."

"I remember when Scipio rode him in those country races a year ago," said Nick. "He won both."

"Cornfield races, with crossbred nags, but swift for their sort," said Booth.

That morning, Saul heated the forge fire and made new shoes to

33

fit Janus all around. Nick rode him a little way, with Scipio on Penny to observe. They brought him back and filed and altered the shoe on the right front foot, to do away with a hint of dragging. Another turn around the track showed there was no fault in the action, and Scipio brought out Dragoon. Dragoon pranced joyously as he approached.

"He knows he's going to race," said Scipio, reining him. "He looks at Janus and reckons Janus won't be any competition."

"We'll find out," said Nick, bringing Janus to starting position. "A mile for the first time. Give us the signal, Scipio."

They held their mounts, the brown nose of Janus beside the higher sorrel nose of Dragoon. "Go!" cried Scipio, and slapped Dragoon's flank.

At the cry, Janus was off, a jump ahead of taller, longer-stepping Dragoon. Nick twitched the reins to keep him from bursting into full speed. Janus wanted to run, wanted to win.

Away they sped, Janus rattling the hard ground away beneath him. At the first turn, Janus was far enough ahead to lead Dragoon around, but in the back stretch Dragoon strove mightily. His head drew opposite Nick's knee.

"Hi, hi!" shouted Scipio and drummed the sorrel flanks with his heels. Dragoon came almost neck and neck, but then Janus increased his pace a trifle and pulled ahead again.

Crouching forward, Nick watched the action of the shoulders. They bunched and rolled, they seemed splendidly matched in action and power. At the second turn, Janus came around on the inside in front of Dragoon, but Nick did not need to check him. Janus seemed to judge his own power, seemed content to stay only a length ahead.

Around again, along the back stretch again, the far turn, and the home stretch. Janus' hoofs sounded like a swift roll of a drum. Nick reined him in at the end of the mile, well out in front.

"Ha, Scipio, here's a racer!" cried Nick over his shoulder. "We weren't even trying hard."

"Dragoon and I tried, all the way," Scipio confessed as he came alongside.

"I wish we'd held a watch on them," Nick said. "What think you of Janus as he gathers speed?"

"He runs with no great leap or stride," Scipio answered. "His feet

move so fast they look fuzzy. Like a beetle scuttling off a hot plate."

Dismounting, Nick felt Janus at shoulders and knees and cannons. He detected no flinch of tenderness, however slight. Janus stood calm. He nudged Nick's shoulder and whinnied softly.

"Look at him, he knows he won," observed Scipio from his saddle.

Nick stroked Janus' neck. "Brave horse," he said. "True, Dragoon is long-winded and may be better at greater distance. Let's jog them along the paths, and after noon dinner we'll have another test."

That afternoon, Booth and Saul both watched. They cheered loudly as Janus ran ahead of Dragoon, two miles this time, and came in under a pull.

"Our Janus runs nobly, Nick," praised Booth, "and nobly you have brought him along. He leaves Dragoon well behind, and Dragoon doesn't like it a whit."

"Scipio rides heavier than I do," reminded Nick. "Tomorrow he shall ride Janus, while I take Dragoon."

On the following day, even with Scipio's greater weight up, Janus twice ran two miles far ahead of Dragoon. Booth watched again, with his son George and Mrs. Armistead. All applauded. Nick led Janus back to the stables, stroking his flank and praising him. Saul fetched out a great piece of toasted bread dipped in warm ale to reward Janus. All watched as Janus consumed this dainty and then went to his manger for twists of dried corn blades.

"He'd win a county race tomorrow," said Mrs. Armistead in her emphatic way. "Upon my soul, son-in-law, you and Nick have done well with him."

"Nay, 'tis Nick more than I," said Booth. "When I think back on it, I realize I've done little beyond buying him and trusting to Nick."

"My trust was in a piping hot Virginia summer," said Nick, mopping his brow. "What Janus had in his shoulder must have been a rheumatism of sorts, and the warmth drove it out. Wipe him down well, Saul, and put his blanket on him."

Janus whinnied softly at his manger. Nick smiled at him.

"Ha, Janus, tomorrow you shall rest and play. No reason to overtrain you, now you're sound again."

Gloucester County's autumn court week came in September. People from the small homes and great, throughout the whole countryside, gathered at the courthouse. Not only were there lawsuits, tax matters, and property deeds to settle; friends met and chatted, farmers traded horses and sold produce, young men and girls said gay commonplaces to each other. On Saturday, with all legal business done, no less than three horse races were run on the mile track beyond the courthouse.

There was a quarter race, quickly run and won. Then came a race of mile heats, with crossbred horses. Booth sat Dragoon to watch, and Nick heard him lament that he had not entered Dragoon. But then blooded horses came to the post, for a single heat of four miles. Booth and Nick spoke to the owners. Most loudly confident among them was Colonel William Byrd.

"I have entered Valiant, and I wager as I wagered four years ago," he announced. "Five hundred pistoles on Valiant, against any horse who challenges. Come, sirs, where's your confidence?"

"Done with you, Colonel," said John Tayloe, handing a purse to the stakeholder. "My Sunrise is son of Traveller, and I have more gold if Mr. Joseph Morton will sell me Traveller this day."

"Not I, in sooth," promptly rejoined Joseph Morton, of Leedstown on the Rappahannock. "Traveller won and won for me, ere I retired him in 1751 to breed me other good racers. There's my Black Marquis, and here's my money on him against Valiant."

The fourth horse in the race was a mare belonging to John Spotswood, whose Newpost plantation was another center of horse-breeding on the Rappahannock. The starter called all entries to the post. They fidgeted and pranced in line, their active little riders dragging hard on the reins. Along the outer and inner edge of the track thronged hundreds of watchers, mounted and afoot. Then the tap of the drum, and away they went.

Sunrise took the lead around the turn and along the back stretch, with the others bunched behind. Nick craned his neck to watch the action of eight striding, flashing pairs of legs. At the start of the second mile, Sunrise and Valiant were neck and neck. They forged ahead of the others and fought for position all the way around the track again. Morton's Black Marquis made a brief bid for first place but fell back, while Spotswood's mare brought up the rear. Halfway around the last time, Valiant wore his way ahead of Sunrise. He was a neck ahead at the final turn and in the home stretch won decisively, to a thunder of cheers. Byrd smiled happily as he took the wagered purses and dropped them into the pockets of his riding coat.

"Congratulations," said Booth, shaking Byrd's hand.

"Praise rather my Valiant," replied Byrd, shaking his elegantly queued head. "Gentlemen all, I'd back him against any horse in these colonies, North or South."

"And you'd be right to do so," vowed Tayloe. "Valiant fairly ran my poor Sunrise into the ground. I'll train him more zealously and try again."

"All horses ran well," said Mordecai Booth. "I mourn that I could send no entry to match with them."

Colonel Byrd took a pinch of snuff from his glittering box and then held it out to his friends. "Ha, Mr. Booth," said he, "I'd thought you might make something of that short-legged creature you brought from England. What's his name again?"

"Janus," volunteered Nick.

"Aye, Janus," Byrd repeated. "Named for the Roman god with faces front and rear. What does the name signify?"

"Mayhap that he'll need a second face to look back on those who run behind him," said Booth, laughing, and Byrd laughed too.

"I race Valiant at Yorktown, the end of this month," he said. "Find speed for your Sunrise, Colonel Tayloe, and fetch along your Janus, Mr. Booth. Valiant and I mean to take purses and victories for years to come."

Nick did not go with Booth to that Yorktown race meeting, nor to visit in Williamsburg afterward. He sat in Booth's office room at Belleville most of that week, reckoning up columns of figures. He was happy to see that all harvests had been good. Belleville showed profits on tobacco, corn, timber, and beef.

Each day he found time to visit the stables. Janus had been exercising less vigorously and seemed to put on flesh. In mid-October, when Booth and his wife and son went for a visit to Byrd's Westover plantation on the James, Nick began to ride Janus again. He galloped Janus briskly morning and afternoon, paying close attention to his every move. The weather grew cooler, but Saul and Nick saw with relief that no stiffness returned to that right shoulder.

"He's cured, Master Nick, and he'll stay cured," predicted Saul. "We must keep him warm all winter though."

Nick had just dismounted after a gallop. He undid the girth buckle and freed Janus from saddle and saddle cloth. He cleared away lather with the sweat knife and found a cloth to rub down the chestnut-brown flanks and legs, the speckled hindquarters, and the strong, clean-tapering neck. He examined the hoofs for possible cracks or lodged pebbles.

"You're glooming, Master Nick," remarked Scipio, strolling near.

"I remember the four miles I saw run last month at Gloucester track," said Nick. "How handily Colonel Byrd's Valiant won, and how Colonel Byrd gloried in him. That's the horse we must plan to beat."

"Aye, Mrs. Armistead tells us that over and over," nodded Saul. "Her heart's set on it. But how would Janus do at four miles?"

"We'll begin to find out, tomorrow morning," Nick decided suddenly. "We'll train him as for a true race. Put him on the training diet again, corn blades and cracked corn and husked oats."

For sixteen days they exercised Janus to bring him back to condition. They began with brief, easy runs, increasing distances and speeds. On the seventeenth morning, Nick walked along the row of stalls.

"Which of these horses run well, other than Dragoon?" he asked. "I want four spry gallopers, none of your amblers like Penny. Aye, and another rider like Scipio."

Scipio pointed out several horses as fairly good runners. "As to riders, there's young Lartius," he said. "He's been helping us at the stables, and I've shown him how to start a horse and bring it along."

Lartius was hailed. He was fourteen years old, dark as molasses and lean as a musket. His big hands seemed knowing as he helped saddle and bridle the four horses. These were all vigorous, clean-limbed beasts, taller by inches than Janus. Saul helped lead them to the track, while Nick rode ahead.

"Lartius, choose a horse and start with me," Nick ordered. "No, leave Dragoon for Scipio to ride the last of four miles. Here's how we'll race: Lartius will ride a mile with me on the best of these three others. Do your best to come in ahead, Lartius. Scipio, be ready in the saddle as Lartius finishes the first mile. Start and ride your best, whether Janus is ahead or behind. Then Lartius on a fresh horse for the third mile, and finally Scipio on Dragoon for the fourth."

"And Janus will race them all, Master Nick?" asked Saul, his dark face frowning.

"All, for a mile each, while he runs four miles," said Nick emphatically. "Nay, how else can we judge of him? But here comes Mr. Booth to watch."

Booth came to the rail of the track, and nodded approval as the plan was explained. "How will you start them?" he asked Saul.

"This will do for a drum," and Saul held out a bucket and a stick.

"Then to it," commanded Booth, "and ride your best, Lartius."

Saul's stick clanged on the bucket, and the two horses flung themselves forward.

Janus was half a jump ahead. Lartius plied a switch to hurry his horse along, but Janus kept a short lead without any strain. Around they went, and around again, Janus half a length in front. He increased this to a length at the post mark, where Scipio started on a fresh horse while Lartius reined to a halt.

That second mile saw Janus trying just a little harder against the new adversary. He finished slightly in front again, and Lartius was away on the third horse. Nick kept a fair pull on the reins, but did not let Lartius catch up. He slowed Janus appreciably at the end of the third mile. Dragoon, with Scipio up, started the final mile neck and neck with Janus.

Dragoon put himself pluckily to the race. He had watched the other horses running, his blood was up, and he ran faster than any of the three that so far had opposed Janus. He was fresh, too, and Janus had run three swift miles. Dragoon strode splendidly, and Nick, watching him alongside, remembered how Valiant's long, clean legs had covered the Gloucester course.

But Janus was too much for Dragoon. He ran with no difficulty, and surely with no pain in his shoulder. Nick eased his pull, and Janus asserted his power, his speed, to draw away from Dragoon. Around they went, and once more around, and Janus came home two lengths ahead.

Saul threw the bucket in the air and roared his applause. Mordecai Booth, too, shouted and jabbered like a happy boy as Nick trotted Janus to the rail and dismounted. Nick studied Janus thoughtfully. Janus breathed deeply but not laboriously. He held his head high, and his eyes were bright and clear.

"Gad's my life, young Nick, here's a heroic racer at the heroic distance!" Booth cried. "This very moment he could run another four miles against four other good horses and win that, too."

"How did his stride look?" Nick asked.

"He scuttled like a quarter horse, his belly almost to the ground," said Booth. "Where other horses run by a series of great leaps, he flashes along, with shorter steps made faster. It's his great leg muscles, before and behind, and his wind and courage and blood."

He patted Janus on the sweat-darkened flank.

"Do you take good care of him, Nick," Booth urged. "He'll make us proud, and make our rivals ashamed as well."

All that fall, Nick was with Janus in the time he could spare from studies and the keeping of accounts. Janus lived in half training, week in and week out, until the first of December. Then he was given his freedom for the winter, with lazy days in stall or paddock and high feeding of grain and hay.

Christmas fell on a Saturday. The following week, the Booths proclaimed festive hospitality to their friends and neighbors. Among house guests were Colonel Byrd and his grave, graceful lady and Colonel Tayloe and his wife and son. On the Wednesday after Christmas, the house was full of guests for an elaborate dinner at three, with a dance in prospect for that night. With the others at table were friends from near Belleville; the Nelsons from across the York at Yorktown, the Burwells of Gloucester, the Baylors of Newmarket, and the Braxtons of Elsing Green. Also at dinner was Mrs. Armistead, and so was grave young Nancy Tyll.

VI

Recognition at the Dance

The ball would begin at eight o'clock, and Nick dressed carefully. He donned a fine suit of rich, plum-colored cloth that Booth had bought for him in England. The breeches were of a snug court cut, and the coat had tapering tails, cuffs turned back, and frogs at the front. The tight waistcoat came to a fashionable point below Nick's belt. His shirt was elaborately ruffled at throat and wrists. He drew white stockings of heavy silk upon his legs, and slid his feet into black leather slippers, with silver buckles that had belonged to his father.

He looked genteel in the mirror. If his dark hair were powdered, he might look grown up. Well, he'd be seventeen in January, and that was close to maturity. Could he dance well, he wondered. Three years ago, he and George Booth had studied dancing and fencing under the Chevalier de Peyroney at Williamsburg, but he had not frequented dances and balls since then. He went down the outside staircase from his quarters and around through the crisp, clear night to the front door.

Belleville's great ballroom was ready prepared for the evening's festivities. Nick never entered it without thinking that six times around its gleaming floor would be a fair race for horses. It extended from back to front of the house. Each of its two big fireplaces might have roasted a sheep or a hog. The paneled walls were painted a soft ivory white. Gleaming chandeliers overhead and candelabra in brass brackets along the walls held scores of blazing

42

wax tapers. At one end, the dining room doors were closed until supper should be announced at ten o'clock. At the other, the double portals of the drawing room had been slid open. Several older ladies and gentlemen sat at tables there, playing whist and backgammon and loo. To one side of those open doors was a stand with a silver punch bowl as big as a soap kettle and stacks of cups around it. On the other side was set the small platform for the musicians.

Guests were gathering, and the dignified butler of the Booths bowed in new parties at the front door. Some sixty ladies and gentlemen, of all ages and all colors of finery, bowed and chattered to each other. Nick entered and made his best bow to Mrs. Booth and Mrs. Byrd, who stood talking near one of the fires. He spoke to various others, hoping that he sounded polished and mature.

"Upon my salvation, Mrs. Braxton, you partnered me well," Mrs. Armistead was saying at the whist table. "You other ladies, had we wagered here as my son-in-law Booth wagers on races, you'd be left poor as church mice when the church burns to its sills."

The musicians mounted their platform. Saul tuned his fiddle. In his long blue coat and snowy neckband he looked like anything but a stable-wise trainer of horses. Scipio was with him, bearing the small drum on which he could patter intricate rhythms. The third musician had been borrowed from Mrs. Armistead's household, a plump, little fellow named Plautus, with his flute.

"Ready for our evening, I see," said a voice Nick knew. It was Thomas, son of Booth's friend and fellow turfman, William Nelson of Yorktown. Thomas was a year older than Nick, and considerably taller. "Remember how Peyroney taught us to tread a measure, Nick?"

"Aye, and his lessons at foil and broadsword," nodded Nick. "And how he died in Braddock's defeat, as brave as any officer Virginia sent."

"But see yonder, where Miss Nancy Tyll hearkens to the musicians tuning," Thomas changed the subject. "I vow, she looks a very princess."

He hurried toward Nancy, and Nick followed him.

She made an impressive appearance in a dress of green brocade. The full overskirt spread in front to reveal a satin underskirt, heavily embroidered with gold and green threads. From beneath the hem peeped the dainty pointed toes of her slippers, also of green brocade. Double-ruffled lace outlined the neck of the tightly fitted bodice and fell at the cuffs just below Nancy's elbows. Her high-dressed hair was powdered to snowy whiteness. In one gloved hand she carried a beaded net purse.

"May I—," Nick began to say, but Thomas was already asking for a dance, and Nancy smiled dignified acceptance.

"Quadrille, ladies and gentlemen," Saul announced grandly.

Two sets of four came out. The music began, the dancers moved and postured. Nick strolled toward the punch bowl. Mordecai Booth was there, drinking and talking with several gentlemen. All of them were richly clad and frostily powdered.

"We must hope that England will send sufficient troops to dispose of these French and their Indians," said one of the group. He was tall, finely set up and rosy-faced. His voice had an elegant precision. Nick did not know him; or perhaps he did, and could not think who he was.

"I'd rather fight them with Americans," declared Colonel William Byrd, sipping. "Look back in your thoughts to poor Braddock's blunders. The king's troops don't always know how to fight in America."

"To some that might sound like disloyalty," said the first speaker, while Nick admired the beautiful cut of his blue coat.

"Sir, do you call me disloyal?" demanded Byrd quickly.

"Never that, Colonel. Yet there's murmur and outcry against King George and the Parliament throughout these provinces. How if treason were charged, and the British came in their regiments to put it down? Your colonials cannot drill like those regulars."

"Pray heaven it never happens," Byrd replied, "but if our American troops drill worse than the British, they shoot better."

"I would mourn such a war," said Booth, holding out his cup to the servant for more punch. "Yet should it come, I feel as does Colonel Byrd—the king's troops don't know how to fight in America."

"These are but jests, gentlemen, and bad ones," put in Tayloe, raising his own cup of punch. "To King George, God bless him!"

All the gentlemen drank to that. Nick watched the dancing of the quadrille. Certainly Thomas Nelson had lost none of the dancing skill he had learned from Peyroney, and Nancy was a tall, sure flow of grace. The music stopped, and Saul bowed from the platform. The dancers applauded themselves. In the drawing room, Mrs. Armistead happily proclaimed another victory at whist. Nick strolled to join Thomas and Nancy, murmuring compliments.

"Many watchers had their eyes upon you, Tom," Nancy told him.

"Not upon me, but upon you," Thomas protested gallantly. "Your silk gown, too, is lovely."

"The brocade came from England," said Nancy. "My cousin, Mrs. Armistead, chose it for me from Mr. Booth's last shipment. She made the sewing woman rip it out thrice ere it was fitted upon me to her taste."

"She's a lady will ever have her way in all things," smiled Nick. "But I crave your favor of the next dance, Nancy."

"Minuet, ladies and gentlemen!" proclaimed Saul, setting his fiddle to his dark chin, and Nancy smiled and gave Nick her hand.

Nick followed the slow, stately intricacies of the minuet, hoping that he kept time. He dared not hope that he was graceful. Nancy was assured and skillful. At the end he bowed ceremoniously, and Nancy dipped low in a curtsey. Mrs. Armistead looked up from her cards to shout approval.

"Sweetly danced and notably, young people," she praised them. "Colonel Washington himself could not have done it better, Nick. Watching the two of you, I remembered my own minuet days, fifty years gone."

Another partner came to lead Nancy away, Lewis Burwell, a Gloucester neighbor of the Booths. Nick returned to the group by the punch bowl. They still spoke of politics and provincial arguments.

" 'Twould be better for us, I opine, if England sent us only good soldiers," Tayloe remarked. "Fewer felons and paupers as settlers, at least."

"Amen to that, sir," agreed the ruddy man in blue. "And perhaps fewer incompetents to hold high office. Governor Dinwiddie, for example—"

"Nay, he does his best," argued Byrd. "I like him well, for all he wrote the king that our House of Burgesses seems too Republican for his tastes."

"He's ever cordial when I see him," added Tayloe.

Nick only half heard as he watched the dancers. Lewis Burwell partnered Nancy in a lively reel. Nick had always admired Burwell's sense about horse racing, but just now he wished that Burwell was less sure and jaunty at dancing. At the end of the reel, Nick was swift to ask Nancy for the next. This time the measures seemed to pass far too quickly.

When the musicians lowered their instruments, Burwell was there, and with him the tall gentleman in blue. Nick bowed himself away as Burwell made introductions and the stranger led Nancy out for a gavotte, livelier than the minuet. Back at the punch bowl, Nick took a full cup from the servant. The conversation had turned to horses.

"Upon my immortal soul, Mr. Booth, I remember when you had a whole squadron of fleet horses to race," Colonel Byrd was saying. "Now they're all gone, save that poor crippled beast from England you showed me earlier this year. What's his name again?"

"Janus," Mordecai Booth said, "and he's no more a cripple. But here's Nick to bear me out that Janus is fully healed."

"Mr. Booth is right, Colonel Byrd," Nick ventured to say. "He has overcome his lameness. We've cared for him our best, and wonders were done by our warm summer."

"Gad's life, Master Nick, say you so?" cried Byrd in good-humored incredulity. "Booth, this astounds me. Next you'll be saying that Janus is as good as ever he was."

"I won't say that he's as good," answered Booth gravely. "I'll say rather that he's better."

The others all began talking excitedly, drowning out the music of the gavotte. They wanted to know all about Janus and his return to health and swiftness. Booth and Nick did their best to answer questions.

"Sirs, this is a wondrous tale," Byrd said, "and I'd hear it with dread, did I not know that my Valiant can outrun any four legs in Virginia."

"Your opinion is your own, Colonel," said Booth, "and an honest one to boot. Yet I take leave to call it but an opinion, and not yet proven."

Byrd stared, then grinned. "What, sir, do you suggest that your scampering little Janus could run against Valiant?"

"I do," said Booth, nodding emphatically. "I'll say here and now, that he might well run against Valiant. Aye, and leave him behind ere the running was over."

Booth and Byrd faced each other like two adversaries. Both were sturdy, strong-faced, assured. Finally Byrd laughed aloud and smote his hands together.

"Boldly said, Mr. Booth," he chuckled, "and plainly meant, I am sure. You make me eager to see our two racers matched."

"I'm as eager as you," rejoined Booth, and all the others listened with rapt interest. "Four-mile heats, Colonel."

"Then let's agree, and at once," said Byrd. "What track, sir?"

"Choose one that's in easy reach of here and your own West-over," suggested Booth.

"What say you both to the Williamsburg course?" suggested Burwell.

"Zounds, the very place," Byrd said. "As for a proper time, why not next April, when the court sits in Williamsburg?"

Booth knitted his brows. "I say rather in June, when the General Assembly meets."

Byrd chuckled again. "These many years I've known your way of thinking, old friend," he said. "You'd prefer June's warmth, because your Janus is so lately recovered from his lameness."

Booth smiled, too. "Some such notion crossed my mind."

Tayloe was at the punch bowl. "Suffer me to give advice," he spoke up. "Colonel Byrd wants the race in April, Mr. Booth in June. What better compromise than to hold it in May?"

"I am willing if Colonel Byrd is," said Booth.

"The very thing," agreed Byrd heartily.

"Then all fill and drink to this good meeting." Tayloe lifted his own cup high. "Gentlemen," he said, "I give you Valiant against Janus, Janus against Valiant, and may the best horse win as he deserves."

"Valiant will do just that," declared Byrd.

They all drank, and Nick drank with them. He decided to be at the stables early next morning to look narrowly at Janus.

"And now, what stakes?" Booth inquired.

"How like you the sound of five hundred pounds?" Byrd asked him.

"Five hundred," Booth repeated. "Agreed, Colonel."

"And in pounds sterling," Byrd elaborated.

"Agreed," said Booth again, and he and Byrd clasped hands in ready agreement.

The others all began to talk again, about Janus and Valiant and horses in general, about the race just agreed upon, and about other races they had seen. Nick listened and thought his own thoughts, but spoke only when someone asked him a question. In the midst of all this, the music stopped. Mrs. Booth came across the floor and spoke to her husband.

" 'Tis nearly ten," she said. "Time for supper."

"Aye, tell Saul to announce it."

Mrs. Booth went to the stand where the musicians waited, and spoke to Saul. Scipio rattled his sticks on his drum to call the attention of the roomful of guests.

"Ladies and gentlemen," Saul addressed them, "supper will be served."

Two other servants were drawing open the double doors. There stood a long table, spread with a white cloth and heaped with platters and bowls of food. At one end was stationed a majestic Virginia ham, which Mordecai Booth began to slice with a huge knife. At the other end, two roast turkeys waited on a broad silver tray. There were pyramids of glasses of jelly, and plates of cakes, meat pies, puddings, tarts. Murmurs of hungry approval rose throughout the ballroom.

Nick looked around for Nancy. He caught the green of her dress as she moved among the others, and hurried to her side.

"May I take you to supper?" he asked.

"I regret to say that you may not, young sir," answered the tall man in blue. "Miss Tyll has graciously accepted my own invitation just now."

"Nick, permit me to present you to Captain Cowles," Nancy smiled. "Mr. Nick Forrest, Captain."

"Servant, sir," said the Captain grandly.

But Nick was staring at him with wide eyes, in which recognition began to dawn. "Captain," Nick repeated. "Captain Cowles, did you say?"

The red face gathered into a smile. "Aye, that's my name. Have we met before?"

"Captain," said Nick again. "No, sir, we've not met before. But I have seen you before and heard you called Captain."

"Captain Cowles was at that race we saw in Gloucester," reminded Nancy. "Do you remember? 'Twas there you saw him."

"Aye, so I did," said Nick hurriedly, "but I saw him once before that. I remember now. 'Twas in Yorktown last summer, when I was just ashore from the voyage from England. Colonel Washington spoke to you then, sir, and he called you, not Captain Cowles, but Captain Magworth."

The captain drew himself stiffly straight, to tower over Nick. His red face seemed to fade to pink.

"You mistake me, young sir," he said harshly.

"No, no, I've wondered where it was I had seen you," Nick said, and his voice sounded sharp and loud in his own ears. "Colonel Washington called you Captain Magworth. And he called you cheat and swindler, too, and bade you never to let him see your face again."

VII

The Making of an Enemy

In his sudden excitement of recognition, Nick had forgotten that he was at a ball among ladies and gentlemen. His voice rang out as though in a stable yard, and everybody turned and stared.

"Nick, you forget yourself," Nancy was saying.

"Nay, I do but remember," returned Nick, eyes on the captain.

"Are you mad, Nick?" Lewis Burwell demanded, striding close. "Captain Cowles is my guest. I have never heard any such charge against him."

"Then hear it now," said Nick. He feared he was not being gentlemanly, he wished he had drawn the captain apart to accuse him, but there was no turning back now. "If he's your guest," Nick went on, "then you don't know him well enough to forbid him your doors."

"We met at Baltimore, he was introduced to me by Colonel Tasker," insisted Burwell. "Captain Cowles—"

"He's not Captain Cowles," broke in Nick. "Captain Magworth is his name. One of his names, anyway."

The captain squared his shoulders. His eye gleamed at Nick. "You're but a boy, and a loud-mouthed, lying boy at that," he said.

"I heard what Colonel Washington said to you last June," Nick told him, very conscious of all the gazes, of all the listening ears. "I stood across the street in Yorktown when he accused you and ordered you out of his sight."

51

The captain's big fists clenched, and Nick shifted his feet to bob away from a blow. But another voice rose, high and loud.

"Nick's right to tell us these things!" Mrs. Armistead shrilled, hurrying across the floor. "If Colonel Washington accused this man—"

" 'Twas a false charge," blurted out the captain.

"Not if Colonel Washington brought it," Mrs. Armistead trumpeted. "I've known him since he was a child, and he never lied in his life, nor has Nick."

"Ladies and gentlemen, I recognize this fellow," came the bass voice of William Nelson of Yorktown as he approached. "His name is indeed Magworth, and Governor Dinwiddie dismissed him from our Virginia service for his dishonesties."

Captain Magworth raked Nick with fierce eyes. "You're young, but not too young to be insolent," he growled. "And not too young to suffer for insolence."

"Fasten no quarrels upon Nick, sir," Colonel Byrd warned Magworth from behind Nelson's shoulder. "Here you stand before us, unmasked as false in name and in character. Deny it if you dare."

Burwell caught Byrd's arm. "I pray you, Colonel, let me speak. My guest is my responsibility. Captain, you and I will depart at once."

Magworth still fixed his hard, bright eyes upon Nick. He swelled inside his elegant blue coat. His face was dark red, except for a bloodless pallor around the tight lips. Then he whirled on his heel and fairly darted for the door. Burwell followed him out.

Everybody began to buzz, to ask questions, and to wonder aloud what the whole story was. Thomas Nelson came close to Nick.

"I judge that you've made an enemy, and a bitter one withal," said Thomas in Nick's ear. "If ever I saw murderous anger on a face, that face belonged to Captain What's-his-name."

Nick said nothing. His strongest feeling was one of embarrassment that he had made a scene before this holiday gathering of gentlefolk. A hand touched his arm. He looked around into Nancy Tyll's grave face.

"You've driven my supper partner away," she said.

"I'm sorry," said Nick, embarrassment coming upon him.

"Not I, though. I'm glad he's gone. May I accept your invitation?"

Burwell appeared at Belleville next morning, as the Booths and their guests sat at breakfast. Nick was there, and the Byrds, the Nelsons, and the Tayloes, and Mrs. Armistead and Nancy.

"Sit with us and drink some coffee," Booth greeted Burwell.

But Burwell stood and looked unhappy. "I hurried over to apologize for my error yesterday in bringing that fellow to the dance."

"We were disappointed that you did not return," Booth said. "We danced until two this morning."

"I was occupied with him," Burwell explained. "He cursed as we went home, and wanted me to bring a challenge to Nick. I told him plainly I'd carry no message from his hand; and though I'd turn no living creature from my house on so cold a night, I expected him to find his way out as early as possible. This morning, the stableman said that the captain saddled his horse at three by lantern light. We shall not see him again."

He went on to tell how, a month before, he had been in Baltimore and had dined with Colonel Tasker. Booth and Tayloe grimaced at the name, remembering how Tasker's mare Selima had beaten their horses in 1752. Burwell said that at Tasker's club he had met Magworth, who called himself Cowles and had talked entertainingly about racing in England. Burwell had said he would be happy to see Captain Cowles at his home. The captain had arrived there two days before the ball, on his way to Edenton in North Carolina.

"And I bade him stay, and last night he came here with me," Burwell finished unhappily.

"You aren't at fault," Booth said generously. "You knew only good of him."

"Aye," agreed Byrd. "If we were all to mourn for how we have misjudged strangers, then we'd sit by regiments in sackcloth and ashes. I, for one, hold no bad feeling against you, Burwell."

"Nor I, nor any here," seconded Booth. "Again, sit with us and let Mrs. Booth pour you coffee. 'Tis fresh roasted and fresh ground and fresh boiled."

When breakfast was finished, Nick said he would go to the stables. The other gentlemen declared they would go with him, and put on greatcoats and cocked hats. The December sun was in a cold gray sky, and frost crackled under their feet as they tramped along the path.

Saul brought out Janus, who was protected against the chill with a blanket strapped over his back and sides and a hood that covered his head and neck so that only his muzzle, ears, and eyes were visible. At Booth's word, Saul led Janus back and forth in the yard while the onlookers watched closely.

"No lameness there, at least while he walks," commented Tayloe.

"Nor while he runs," said Nick. "Halt him, Saul. Now, if you will, look at his right front hoof—'tis flat and firm to the ground."

Stooping, Nick lifted the hoof into his lap. "And the shoe is worn evenly, and not all at the toe," he pointed out, tapping the iron with his finger. "He favors this foot no more."

"Set it down again, Nick," said Booth, and lifted the other front foot. "This shoe is worn evenly with the other."

"Might you have shod his feet at different times?" suggested Byrd.

"Never with Janus," Nick assured him. "We shoe him all around each time."

Tayloe stroked Janus' hooded neck and thrust his hand under the blanket. "The right shoulder, you say? He flinches no whit when I rub it."

At Booth's word, Saul led Janus back to his stall. Then Booth and Nick unstrapped and drew off the heavy blanket, and Saul held a lantern high while all of them examined Janus.

"He looks in high flesh," observed Burwell.

"He's been eating well, and we've kept him to easy paces," said Nick. "Brisk work will bring him into prime condition, and he will not have gone stale."

Colonel Byrd paced all the way around Janus, his plump face thoughtful. He slapped the withers, the flank, the mottled haunch. "Hmmm," Byrd crooned. "There's power in those bones and muscles, Mr. Booth."

"Aye, so there is," agreed Burwell enthusiastically. "In barrel and quarters he's as well set as your own Valiant, Colonel."

"The difference is in their legs," went on Byrd, his hand on the nape of Janus' neck. "Fourteen hands and but a hair more, as I judge. Now, Valiant stands sixteen hands and two inches—ten inches higher, gentlemen, with most of that height in the leg. He'll outstep Janus with every stride."

"Janus may stride faster," Nick said boldly, and Byrd smiled.

"Youth's enthusiasm," Byrd drawled. "Stride is what will win at the heroic distance, Nick. Mr. Booth, we've already wagered at even money, you and I, for we are the owners. But I'll be generous. Eight to five on Valiant against this Janus next May at Williamsburg."

"Done, Colonel," said William Nelson promptly. "One hundred pistoles in gold on Janus, at that figure. I'm a York River dweller, and so is Janus, by reason of the Ware running down into the York. So I stand with him against you and Valiant, champions of the James."

Byrd fished out a pocketbook and pencil and jotted down the wager as though he was in no financial trouble from his other lost bets. "Any others at eight to five?" he challenged.

"We've months in which to accept you, sir," said Burwell. "I may fetch money for Janus to carry against you at that meeting."

"You'll be welcome," nodded Byrd. "Valiant has strength and speed to bear fortunes on himself, all the way to victory."

Nick drew his coat about him and put on warm gloves. "Saddle Janus," he told Saul. "I'll see how he runs this chilly morning, and other mornings to come. Make him a warm mash for breakfast when we come back."

"Would I might stay to watch," said Byrd, "but tomorrow I must wait on Governor Dinwiddie in Williamsburg, to talk of the French war and what Virginia will do in it."

"No better man could the governor call to advise him," Booth said honestly.

He and Byrd strolled back toward the house in the rosy morning light. The other guests followed. Saul finished saddling Janus, and Nick mounted and rode out northward into a chill breeze.

Nick paid careful attention to Janus' performance, that day and the days that followed. Cold weather had not stiffened the healed shoulder. Nick used only spoken commands, without whip or spur, but Janus seemed eager to run. Nick and Saul supervised Janus' feeding. Exercise brought a gradual hardening of muscles and a loss of some plumpness.

January 11 was Nick's seventeenth birthday. At breakfast that morning, Mordecai Booth told him to give Janus a rest.

"I want you with me today," said Booth, "and tomorrow. We go to Yorktown, then to Williamsburg."

"Gladly, Mr. Booth, if I can be of help to you," agreed Nick.

"Maybe we'll help each other, lad," said Booth, and went out to order saddles on Dragoon and stout, ambling Penny. Nick packed his valise and donned riding boots, heavy coat, and gloves.

Snow fell lightly from gray clouds as they rode down to Gloucester Point on the York. They arrived before noon, and a great ferry barge took them across to Yorktown. There Booth spent some hours talking with his clerks. Nick checked figures on sales and inventories, remembering how he had first seen Captain Magworth on the street outside. It was late afternoon and still snowing when they left Yorktown for Williamsburg a dozen miles away. They arrived at sunset and dismounted at the great Raleigh Tavern. Stablemen took charge of the horses and landlord Alexander Finnie welcomed them.

"I'll buy you a good birthday dinner, Nick," said Booth. "Tomorrow we have important business here in Williamsburg."

"I hope it turns out to your profit, sir," said Nick.

"And to yours," Booth replied, smiling.

But that was all that he would say about their Williamsburg errand, that night or next morning at breakfast. They ate and went out in the street, to see shopkeepers brushing the snow from in front of their doors on Duke of Gloucester Street.

"Come, we'll go afoot," said Booth, beckoning Nick to come with him to the westward along the brick walk.

They strolled past shops, past another tavern, the Market Square and the green of the Governor's Palace. The Bruton Parish Church stood silent and tall to the right of their way. At last they crossed a street and went through a gate in a low brick wall. Beyond stood several buildings, also of brick.

"This is the College," said Nick. "William and Mary."

"Aye," nodded Booth, "and our business is yonder, at that house."

They went to the broad front door, and Booth swung the knocker. A Negro woman in a white cap opened to them.

"Mr. Booth?" she asked. "And Mr. Forrest? Come in, sirs. You can hang your coats in the hall here. The president's awaiting you, in his study."

They entered and hung up their greatcoats. Nick earnestly wanted to ask what they were doing there, but Booth had not said a

word about it. The woman opened an inner door of oak. In the
room beyond, Nick saw shelves of books, a paper-strewn desk, and
a man rising to greet them. He was of medium size and build, with
gray-sprinkled hair and a dark scholar's gown.

"Good morning, Mr. Booth," he said, taking off a pair of
square-lensed spectacles and shaking Booth's hand.

"Servant, Mr. Dawson," said Booth. "May I present my young
friend Nicholas Forrest? Nick, this is President Dawson, of the
College."

"Draw up chairs, if you will," said Dawson, sitting down again
and picking up a paper. "Here's your letter, Mr. Booth, and here's
the young gentleman of whom you have written." He put on the
spectacles again and studied the letter. "Seventeen years old, I see."

"He reached that venerable age but yesterday," said Booth.

"And these are reports of his earlier schooling," Dawson continued, "but how of his studies this last year and the one before?"

"He and my son pursued those at my home," Booth replied.

Dawson studied Nick, levelly but kindly. "Suppose we find out a
few things about those studies," he said. "Mr. Forrest, will you
favor me by construing a page or so of Latin?"

He handed Nick an open book. Nick saw with relief that it was
Plutarch, whose works he had read that very winter.

"Here's the life of Themistocles, sir," said Nick. "He jokes with
his son." Knitting his brows, he translated: " 'The Athenians rule
Greece, and I rule the Athenians, and your mother rules me, and
you rule your mother.' "

"Well enough," approved Dawson, "though I apprehend the passage isn't strange to you. Go on from there."

Nick did so, for the rest of the page and another. Dawson then
handed him a volume of Vergil, and Nick translated some lines of
the *Aeneid,* not too lamely.

"He has a good acquaintance of Latin," Dawson said. "How is
his Greek?" He offered another volume. "Can you read the author
and the title?"

Nick studied the characters. " 'Tis *Oedipus the King,* by Sopho-
cles," he said.

"Right. Let us hear you read from it."

Nick did his best, slowly and cautiously. At last Dawson held up
his hand.

"Bravely tried, at least," he granted. "Your Greek and Latin foundations can be built upon, with study. What of your mathematics?"

"I'll speak to that," volunteered Booth. "He keeps skillful accounts for my plantation and my trade."

"Let him try these examples," said Dawson. "Draw your chair to the desk, Mr. Forrest, and dip pen in ink."

He laid a sheet of paper before Nick. It bore ten equations in algebra and ten problems in geometry. As Nick went to work, he half-heard Booth and Dawson chatting about the weather, politics, English trade, tobacco prices, horses, manners, school matters. An hour passed. Nick sweated as though at hard work or play.

"Have you done?" Dawson asked finally.

"I cannot finish the last equation, sir," Nick confessed.

"Tell me that in French."

Nick did so, not too stumblingly, and Dawson asked him other questions in French, to which Nick replied. At last Dawson smiled.

"I think you'll do well at this college," he said.

Nick stared, and Mordecai Booth chuckled.

"I kept you in darkness, lad, lest you worry all yesterday and all last night," he explained. " 'Twas ever your father's wish that you be educated here. To that end I've made you study and learn. Now Mr. Dawson says you may enter; and so you shall, at my charge. That's my birthday present to you."

"Let him come next fall, Mr. Booth," said Dawson. "Will you take dinner with us? There are some sixty young gentlemen enrolled. Mr. Forrest may want to meet some who'll be his fellow scholars."

"I can't think how to say my thanks," Nick said to Booth. "How can I show them?"

"Janus waits at Belleville," Booth reminded him. "He, too, must have his test and triumph. Prepare him, as you were prepared for this entry into a gentleman's education. Prepare him to earn rewards and conquer enemies."

"Enemies," Dawson said after him. " 'Tis hard to believe that young Mr. Forrest is troubled by enemies."

Nick said nothing. He was thinking of Captain Magworth.

VIII

The New Rider

Back at Belleville, Mrs. Booth and George joyfully heard the news of Nick's acceptance for entrance into the College of William and Mary. Both of them offered congratulations and predicted brilliant things for him.

"I'd be going with you, Nick, but my ambition is to be a planter," said George. "And too, I look for a commission in one of our Virginia regiments."

Saul and Scipio, too, rejoiced with Nick, but said that they would miss him.

"Who'll train Janus if you become a scholar?" Saul asked.

"I'm no scholar yet," said Nick, "nor shall I be until fall. As to Janus, let's take him for a gallop tomorrow."

The next day was bright but bitter cold. Nick rode Janus out to the exercise track and put him to a canter, then a swift surge of speed. Janus ran willingly, but a hint of irregularity in his gait made Nick frown.

He checked Janus to a slower pace, and brought him in after only a short while. He and Saul massaged the right shoulder that once had been lame.

"Winter has touched him in the old spot, I fear," said Nick. "If he is run too hard, he may strain the tendon again. Let's mix a hot poultice and make the blood flow swift and strong there."

To such treatment, Janus responded, but Nick was cautious

61

about extending him to any great effort. He and Saul and Booth all yearned for warm weather again.

When Mrs. Armistead next visited Belleville with Nancy Tyll, they were told the news of Nick's acceptance at the College. Both surprised Nick by their responses.

"I daresay, ma'am, that you think Nick should bide here and tend horses," Booth suggested to his mother-in-law.

"Not I," stoutly rejoined the old lady. "There's far more for a bright young man to learn than even a wise horse may tell him. Sure, Nick has learned as much concerning horses as anyone of his age I ever knew. Now it's time that he finds out if he can rein and ride the books."

"There's a whole world for me to know of," Nick agreed modestly.

"Aye, when you study Alexander and his conquests, you'll read about his great horse Bucephalus, for whom he named a town," Mrs. Armistead lectured him. "And in your Latin, there'll be report of how the Romans raced in their great circus—driving chariots, so I've heard tell, and it must have been wondrous to watch them. As for the Greeks, there àre other noble tales of horses and how they ran, even how Pegasus flew to the heights of heaven." Her old eyes danced as they looked at Nick. "Tell me," she said, "will they let you keep a horse of your own at that College of William and Mary?"

Nancy was grave, almost moody, as she and Nick sat apart that afternoon.

"And have you dreamed of this, Nick?" she asked him. "Have you thought of college your life long?"

"Nay, it never occurred to me I might go," he replied. "Therefore I never dreamed of it, for I felt there was no use to dream."

"What would it be like to go to a college, learn the wisdom of ancient times and modern?" Nancy seemed to muse. "If you never wondered, I have. And often."

"You have thought of going to college!" Nick cried out in shocked amazement. "But girls do not go to colleges, such a thing was never heard of."

"I know," Nancy agreed gravely. "My cousin Armistead has seen that I have had tutors to give me education, and I have read books such as colleges give their students. I've been schooled beyond what most girls expect, I suppose. Otherwise, I can play the spinet, I can embroider and sew, I can say a few things in French. That is enough, I suppose, for any girl."

Nick stared at her in confusion. He felt as though he was being charged with some selfish act.

"Nancy," he attempted after a moment, "surely you aren't jealous of me. You don't sit there and wish that I would be denied this college education."

"I think I envy you," she told him. "I could even wish that I had been born a boy."

"I am heartily glad that you were born a girl," Nick assured her earnestly, and Nancy's eyes shone.

"I had not thought of how I sounded," she apologized. "Perhaps what I had in mind was that you and I have grown greatly since we met last June. You are seventeen now, and I'll be seventeen in March. You seemed like a boy in early summer. Now you seem a man, ready to take your place in the world."

"Come, Nancy," Nick tried to tease her back into a cheerful mood. "When we first met, 'twas you who did the studying, and I struck you as one who knew only about horses. I hazard that what truly vexes you is that I may grow bookish at college and will come and vaunt my learning over you."

"Nay, Nick, that you would never do."

He took her hand, and she let him hold it.

"I have it in mind that I'll miss seeing you as often as now," he said to her. "But I'll come back to Belleville from time to time and will hope to meet you here. We've been good friends, I think, ever since the night of the ball."

"When Captain Magworth was taking me in to supper," she said.

"But it was I who escorted you at last," he reminded. " 'Twas a very good supper indeed, if memory serves me."

He meant to speak lightly, but she did not smile. "Captain Magworth," she said the name unhappily. "He looked at you as though he would kill you outright."

"So he did, but I am still alive."

"Suppose he should come upon you and attack you?"

"I'd fight him if need be," said Nick. "In no case would I run from him."

Mrs. Armistead came where they sat. "Nancy, come play for us," she invited. "A graceful French tune if you will."

Nancy went to the spinet and played sweetly and skillfully. Nick listened with pleasure. But next day, after exercising Janus and treating the troublesome shoulder, he tacked a playing card to a tree behind the stables. Scipio stood with him, to load and reload a pair of duelling pistols. Nick was comforted to find that at ten paces he could hit the card six times out of nine.

On a bright, mild afternoon in mid-February, a visitor rode up to the door at Belleville. He was Robert Page of Broadneck in Hano-

ver County, and an earnest, expert racer of horses. Booth welcomed him cordially and brought him inside, while a servant led Page's riding horse to the stables.

"It is always a pleasure to see you, Mr. Booth, but this is important business as well," said Page, while Nick stood near and listened. The master of Broadneck was a slim, spruce man in his thirties, with a weather-beaten face. From inside his handsome riding coat, he rummaged a folded paper.

"A letter from our mutual friend, Colonel William Byrd of Westover," he said, handing it to Booth. "You may have heard that Lord Loudon is to be named governor general of Virginia and is on his way to America to command our forces against the French. Byrd must perforce give all his attention to his regiment—recruit it and see to its equipment. He will march away north to Pennsylvania. As I am his friend and near neighbor, he asks me to represent him in the matter of the race between Janus and Valiant."

"Aye, so he writes here," said Booth, reading. "And he could not have named an abler proxy, sir."

Mrs. Booth appeared in the room, escorting a maid with refreshments. Booth and Page sat down to coffee and frosted cakes. At Booth's gesture, Nick joined them at the table.

"You and Byrd have exchanged letters, agreeing that you might name good riders for your horses," continued Page.

"True, we did, for both of us ride heavier than when we were young men," nodded Booth, looking at the letter. "I see he's chosen Daniel Lewis to ride Valiant. Mr. Lewis is of a good South Carolina family, and as a good a gentleman rider as I am aware of."

"Who will ride Janus for you?" Page asked.

"I am not yet ready to answer that," said Booth. "Now, since you speak for Valiant, what day shall we race at Williamsburg?"

"I had thought the seventh of May," replied Page. "It is a Saturday, and the General Assembly will be sitting. We can be sure of a crowd to watch, and in it some of the foremost men of Virginia."

"Seventh of May," Booth said after him and dipped pen in ink to note it on a tablet. "Agreed to that, sir. But come, when we finish our coffee, we'll go out and watch Janus as he takes his afternoon gallop."

"Generously offered, Mr. Booth, but I'd be less than fair to join you at that watching," said Page as he rose. "Though we call each other friends, we must get used to thinking of each other as enemies."

"Enemies, sir?" Booth cried. "Never that, in any matter."

"In one matter," insisted Page. "This race. You'll do your utmost, I know, to fetch Janus in a winner. So shall I do my utmost for Valiant. Indeed, I go to Westover tomorrow, and I hope to make a winner of him. I'd never spy on Janus and his weaknesses."

"Weaknesses, say you?" said Booth, also rising. "Zounds, you're already on the way to defeat if you ascribe weaknesses to Janus."

He and Page shook hands heartily.

"Goodbye for the nonce," said Page. "And good fortune in all things, save this race on the seventh of May next."

"Farewell, and never might I call for a better and kinder enemy," Booth rallied him.

But when Page had ridden away, Booth seemed to retire into a dark, meditative mood. He sat by the drawing room fire and smoked a long pipe all the rest of the afternoon. At breakfast on the following day, he announced that he would be gone for several days to Yorktown and to Williamsburg.

"Do you continue with Janus, Nick," he said as he left. "Bring him along in such a way as to heal that shoulder stiffness. You are working wonders with him."

Booth was gone for a week. Nick exercised Janus daily, saw to his feeding and care, with special attention to poultices and hot packs for the right shoulder. Several times, Nick practiced with pistols. It was on February 18, a Friday, that Booth returned. With him was a guest.

"This is Mr. Carr Thane," Booth introduced the stranger to his wife. "Ha, Nick, come and shake a hand worth your shaking. Carr Thane—he has come lately from England. There he has ridden and won on the foremost tracks, and at Christmas time he was a winner in Maryland."

"Honored, Mr. Thane," said Nick, offering his hand.

Thane took it with a brief, hard squeeze. He was smaller even than Nick, though he seemed to be in his middle thirties. He wore an elegant, high-collared overcoat and snug, gleaming boots. In his lean left hand he carried a riding whip like a limber, shiny cane. Its head was a knob of solid silver. His face was dark and bony, with deep, shrewd lines bracketing the hard mouth and seaming the forehead. His eyes seemed to crouch deep in their sockets. They gleamed like bright beads.

"How do you do," said Thane loftily.

"Come, off with your coat," Booth urged him. "Wife, will you order us some spiced wine? 'Twas a cold ride hither from the York. Now, Nick, come sit with us and talk. Mr. Thane was good enough to say he will be our guest and ride Janus in the race."

Nick felt as if icicles suddenly formed in all his arteries and veins. He must have looked blank and miserable, for Booth smiled.

"Nay, lad, take heart," said Booth, clapping Nick's shoulder. "You have trained Janus well, and you'll continue to train him. But for a rider we must have one of full experience and brilliant skill."

"Sir, you overwhelm me," said Thane, but he did not sound overwhelmed.

"His fame has run before him, swifter than any horse," elaborated Booth. "If possible, he rides better than Mr. Daniel Lewis. We may count ourselves lucky to have his help."

" 'Tis I who am lucky," Thane said, as he unbuttoned his big coat and drew it off. "All I've heard these two months is talk of the coming race and of how the world will look on. I'm eager to see your horse and to ponder what to make him do."

With the overcoat off, Thane appeared in tight coat and breeches of blue. His body looked as thin as a sword, and as keenly tempered. Nick judged that Carr Thane was all bone and tendon and sure muscle, with not an ounce of softness anywhere. The spiced wine was brought, and the three sipped and talked.

Thane asked the most penetrating questions and listened to the answers attentively. He smiled at one or two things Nick said. Thane's smile was a strange, hard grimace, with the lips grimly drawn together and the corners of the mouth turned down. At last he drained the final drops of his wine and got to his feet.

"Shall we go visit Janus?" he said, reaching for his coat.

Booth and Nick went out with him. In the stable, Booth ordered Saul to strip the blanket from Janus. Carr Thane entered the stall and walked close to Janus, prodding his back and ribs with skilled fingers. He doubled a hard fist and struck Janus on the right shoulder, and hummed to himself when Janus winced slightly. Pausing in front, Thane stared into Janus' brilliant brown eyes, as though reading a message there.

All the rest of the way around Janus, Thane moved with slow steps. He continued to feel here and there. Sometimes he pressed hard with the heel of his hand or jabbed with a finger. He knelt to examine the legs and lifted the hoofs, one after another.

"Suppose we take him out and see how he runs," Thane suggested at length.

"Nay, he's been exercised hard, both morning and afternoon today," volunteered Nick.

"Indeed?" Thane ran his palm over Janus' shoulder where the neck joined it. "He seems to have borne up well under it. Then let's say early tomorrow."

"As early as you like, Mr. Thane," said Nick.

Thane did not seem to hear him. He spoke to Saul.

"Have bridle and saddle on him at sunrise," Thane ordered. "I'll ride him. The sooner he and I understand each other, the better."

With that, Thane walked out of the stall, out of the stable and back toward the house. He walked as though he owned house, stable, and Janus himself. Booth strolled with him, talking. Nick stayed where he was and watched them go.

"I hope he truly knows what he's about," muttered Nick.

"I hope so, too," said Saul beside him.

IX

Carr Thane's Methods

The morning was mild for February, with misty clouds in the sky. When Nick came to breakfast, Booth and Thane already were sitting at table. On Thane's plate was a thin slice of dark-red ham, from which he carefully sliced all the fat. He wore a short jacket of yellow wool that hugged his leanness from throat to waist. He also had a great mug of black coffee.

The maid brought in more ham and a variety of hot breads. Thane accepted only one pancake and declined butter and honey. He talked about horses to Booth but not to Nick.

When they finished eating and stood up, Nick saw that on Thane's shiny boots were strapped long brass spurs. Their spiked rowels looked as big as silver crown pieces.

"Sir, Janus has been ridden only with light prick spurs here," Nick made bold to say. "I find that he responds better to a word in time than to whip or spur."

Thane looked at Nick, but made no reply. He put on a round black cap with a visor and tucked his silver-knobbed whip under his arm. They all went out to the stable together.

Saul had Janus ready saddled and bridled, and Dragoon was also led out for Booth. Nick chose a mare named Circe, recently bought by Booth from William Nelson. She was a nimble crossbred, brown with white feet.

"Can that mare run fairly well?" Thane asked.

"Aye, and Nick will tell you of her spirit," Booth replied. "Let me say, Mr. Thane, Nick's a lad of true, good horse sense."

"I nothing doubt it," said Thane loftily. "But with this race before us, 'tis high time for a man of horse sense to take charge."

He mounted Janus and took up the reins. The three rode at a walk out to the exercise track.

"And now to warm up," decreed Thane. "Ride with me a little, youngster."

Janus took off easily and readily, and Nick rode alongside. Thane seemed to watch, to listen, and to feel with hands and knees every movement Janus made. Around the track they went, and as they accomplished a lap, Thane called for Nick to increase Circe's pace. Janus would have moved ahead of her, but Thane kept him under check. They finished the lap to where Booth sat and watched on tall Dragoon.

"Out ahead now, and smart's the word," Thane told Nick.

A slap on the shoulder sent the brown mare into a swift burst of speed. As she galloped ahead, Nick looked back at Janus.

Janus was not speeding to catch up. He reared high, with forefeet pawing the air, and Thane dragged on the reins so hard that Janus' mouth gaped open. At once Nick reined Circe around to gallop back. He saw Thane lift his whip high, reversed in his hand, to bring down the silver knob on top of Janus' head. Again Thane lifted the whip and clubbed Janus with it.

Next instant Nick rode so close that Circe's flank drove against Janus. Out darted Nick's hand. He seized the whip and wrenched it from Thane.

"Stop that!" Nick yelled into Thane's face.

Janus went pitching and bucking across the track. Thane fought to stay in the saddle. Nick threw the whip to earth, rode close again, and caught Janus by the bridle, close to the bit. Bright-red blood showed on Janus' mouth.

"Get down off him and tie him to the post there," Nick fairly blazed at Thane. "I'll get down too, and I'll show you how it feels to be beaten about the head."

Thane's gaunt face was a scowling fury. He was out of the saddle in a twinkling, and Nick, too, jumped down upon the track.

But then Mordecai Booth came riding and roaring. He shoved Dragoon in between them.

"In heaven's name, what madness is this?" he thundered down at Nick. "Mr. Thane, what are you doing?"

"This brute you want me to ride sought to throw me off," Thane panted. "Then this young ruffian threatened me, and I'll not stand tamely to hear that."

Nick flung the mare's bridle over the top of a post and tried to come toward Thane under Dragoon's nose.

"You were clubbing Janus with the loaded butt of your whip," he charged. "See him, he's bleeding where you struck him. Come, Mr. Thane, stand out where I can get at you. I'll draw enough blood from you to make things even."

"Silence, Nick!" Booth commanded him angrily. "Mr. Thane, I await your explanation."

"I spurred him——," Thane began to say.

"And I told you he was not used to those great fangs you wear at your heels," Nick broke in. "I told you, and you did not deign to listen."

"Sir," said Booth grimly to Thane, "this isn't good horsemanship."

Thane drew himself up, trying to look tall. "Take thought to whom you speak of horsemanship, Mr. Booth."

"Nay, do you take thought," Booth said swiftly. "I am Mordecai Booth of Belleville, and this is my land, and that is my horse. I told you last night that Nick is trainer of Janus, and that you will ride him. So let it be. But I tell you again, Mr. Thane, give ear to what Nick says about the treatment of Janus."

"I will say this much, even now," Nick spoke up. "Janus will not be ridden a step farther this morning. He has been hurt, and he needs care."

So saying, he walked past Dragoon and took the bridle from Thane's hand. Thane's deep-set eyes glittered dangerously, but Nick led Janus away. Back to the stable they walked together, Nick speaking softly to comfort and calm Janus. Behind him, Nick heard Thane's voice rise in angry protest, and Mordecai Booth's louder shout to interrupt. Into the stall Nick led Janus. He and Saul stripped away bridle, saddle, and saddle cloth. Janus' chestnut flank was cruelly gashed by Thane's rowelling. Nick hurried to dig a handful of astringent salve from a bucket, to spread on the wounds. Saul coaxed Janus into opening his mouth and carefully sponged it out.

Outside came the noise of approaching hoofs, and riders were dismounting. A shadow fell at the stable door. Nick glanced that way and saw Thane coming in.

At once Nick wiped the salve from his hands on a rag of toweling. Then he left the stall. He approached Thane with careful steps, his hands half-clenched at his sides.

"Do not be so warlike, Mr. Forrest," said Thane. "I am here to make my peace with you."

Nick came to a halt at that, two paces away. He said nothing, but watched Thane intently.

"Janus was trying to throw me off," Thane went on. "Indeed, had I not reined him in sharply, I'd have gone over his head."

"There was no need for you to club him with your loaded whip," Nick said bluntly.

"At the moment, I thought there was," Thane said, and smiled his upside-down smile. "But hark you, Mr. Booth told me flatly that I should have paid more attention to what you tried to tell me of Janus. And, when I thought on it coolly, I saw he spoke the truth."

Nick relaxed a trifle. "Well, sir?" he prompted.

"I can see now that I startled Janus when I spurred him so suddenly," admitted Thane. "And sooth to say, he startled me when he began to prance and rear and fight. Now, if I say that I was wrong, is that sufficient? For I want to be friends with you, and also with Janus."

"Come, Nick," said Booth, also entering the stable. "I call that handsomely said on Mr. Thane's part. You're no proper gentleman if you do not accept his words. I stand here, waiting to see the two of you take hands in good spirit to each other."

"Very well," Nick yielded and held out his hand. Thane gripped it briefly, then walked to the stall where Janus stood. Saul was washing the cuts on Janus' head.

Janus flung up his head and reared slightly as Thane approached, but Nick came and spoke to him in quiet tones and stroked his brown neck. As Janus relaxed, Thane also patted and stroked him.

"See, he forgives me," declared Thane. "He acts the part of a true gentleman, and I'll deserve this confidence in me hereafter. No more rowelling for him, from this time forward."

With that, Thane lifted one booted foot, then the other, and unstrapped his heavy spurs.

"Hereafter I'll wear simple nudgers," he said. "How badly did I wound him? I think it was no great injury, after all. He and I must try another run together this very afternoon, to make sure of our good fellowship."

All of which was most handsomely said indeed, Nick told himself. He wished that such talk and manners made him feel friendly toward Carr Thane. Perhaps he still felt a tweak of jealous disappointment that Thane, and not he, would ride Janus against Valiant in the race.

The afternoon's exercising did much to reconcile Janus to Thane. Riding alongside on Circe, Nick heard Thane speaking constantly and encouragingly to Janus.

"You say sooth, Nick, he responds to words and touches as the best of racers respond to whip and spur," Thane said at the end of the ride. "Tomorrow he and I will make even greater speed."

And sure enough, Janus ran better each day with Thane astride him. As March brought warmer weather, the last of that stiffness in the right shoulder departed again, and Janus scuttled around the track so that his hoofs seemed to blur like the wings of a humming-bird. Thane pronounced him worthy to run for the King's Plate itself, against the best horses in England.

In other matters, Thane was mannerly, quiet, and temperate. All noticed how sparingly he ate and drank. He took wine with Booth no oftener than once a week. His drink at table was plain water or black coffee. He ate lean meat and toasted bread, but no sweet cake or pie whatever. This, he explained, was to keep him lean and light for riding. Nick was inclined to imitate him in this moderation at the table.

Mrs. Armistead came calling and brought Nancy with her. Thane delighted the old lady with his talk of great horses and great races watched by the king himself and all his court. Thane told vividly of how he had ridden some of the swiftest horses—both Blank and Cygnet, great sons of the great Godolphin Arabian. Nancy, too, listened with happy eagerness when Thane described a meeting with Henry Fielding. Fielding had written *Tom Jones* and *Joseph Andrews,* favorite novels of Mrs. Armistead and Nancy, and he was a sportsman and a social favorite as well.

By Saturday, April 16, three weeks before the day of the race, Booth, Nick, and Thane agreed that Janus was in fine condition and needed only the finishing touches.

"Then we'll go day after tomorrow to Williamsburg," announced Booth. "My friend Nelson has a small farm a mile or so north of the town, where is a half-mile exercise track. He says we may take Janus there for the last of his training."

"Would I could come, too," said George Booth, "but I'm busied with the spring planting. What are the odds now?"

"Word comes to me that Thane's good riding of Janus has its effect upon the wagering," replied Booth. "Where once Valiant was favored at eight to five, 'tis now even money."

"Part of that change of odds is because Colonel Byrd is not at hand to see to Valiant," suggested Thane.

"That may have had its effect, but I am sure that your presence in the saddle was a chief cause," Booth insisted.

They made the start at midmorning of the following Monday, under blue spring skies with green trees and fields along the roadway. Booth rode Dragoon, Thane rode Penny, and Nick sat on Circe and led Janus by a halter. Saul, too, came with the party, driving a light carriage with luggage and supplies stowed aboard. Down they traveled to the York River and crossed on the ferry. William Nelson met them in Yorktown for dinner and escorted them to his property north of Williamsburg.

" 'Tis no splendid or luxurious place, as you yourself can see," Nelson said to Booth in apologetic tones. "Yet maybe 'twill serve your practical purposes. My heart's with Janus in this race, as well as five hundred pistoles I've wagered upon him."

To Nick, the little farm looked pleasant enough. Most of it was given over to apple orchards, just then budding bravely. The house had been a small, low building of brick, to which had been added a whole new front of weatherboard. The roof was shingled with thick, rough slabs of cedar. Behind the house stood a rough, massive stable, and behind the stable lay a half-mile exercise track.

The party dismounted at the door, and Nelson opened the door and led them in. "Of late this house stood empty, but I ordered it swept out," he said. "From Yorktown I sent over bedclothes and cooking pots and so on. Would you like me to lend you house servants?"

"Do not trouble yourself, pray," Booth answered. "Saul here is as skilled in the kitchen as in the paddock. He'll cook well enough for horsemen to enjoy."

They went through room after room. There were beds in all of them, already made up. Saul paid special attention to the kitchen, where a broad fireplace was furnished with a crane to hang a pot. In the bricks at the side was set the iron door of an oven. On the wall hung copper skillets and gridirons and forks, and on shelves stood stacked dishes and mugs. Saul nodded over these as though satisfied.

"I'll ride into town and send back provisions and other items we need," announced Booth. "Nick, I leave things here in your charge and in Mr. Thane's."

He rode away with Nelson. Nick and Thane led the horses to the stable. Nick chose a stall for Janus. Then they hung up saddles and bridles and harness and explored the feed bins. Finally all three walked out to survey the track.

" 'Tis rough-faced here and there," commented Thane. "Saul, you and I must get rakes and level those ridges and fill those hollows."

They found tools and went to work. Nick returned to the stable. He found a stack of dry corn blades and began to make twists of them. Janus watched from his stall.

"Ha, boy," Nick addressed him. "They count your chances against Valiant as even. But you'll outrun Valiant, and the world will cheer."

Janus bobbed his long head and whinnied as though he understood and agreed.

X

Final Training

Booth returned with great parcels lashed to Dragoon's saddle. There was a sack of meal, a smoked shoulder of pork, a great red beef roast, butter wrapped in a green cabbage leaf, and a pot of jam and other things. Saul cooked a savory supper for them. As usual, Thane ate but sparingly, and so did Nick. Booth, chuckling at their small portions, served himself with as much as the two of them together. All were in bed early.

By common consent, Janus was not exercised next morning.

"Aye, let the brave fellow idle in the stable yard, with Saul to tend him," Booth said. "He had a long journey down from Belleville, though he did not run."

"And we don't want him to overwork," added Thane. "He's near to his best condition even now, and we must keep him there."

"But he must eat only what will keep him to that condition," was Nick's contribution.

And so it was ordered. Nick and Thane and Booth saddled their other horses and rode into Williamsburg to survey the race track.

Set free of the houses and streets of Williamsburg, the track was a great level stretch surrounded by trees. It was a regular oval in shape, twice as long as it was wide, lying east and west. Midway on the stretch that was nearer the town, three tall posts were driven on the track's inner edge to enclose a triangle, and a small platform was built in their midst.

"The judges' stand," Booth informed them, pointing to the posts. "There the race starts and finishes."

78

Other, lower posts were set around the inner border of the track. Nick estimated that these were about five feet high. They were driven at intervals of fifteen feet or so. The inner space confined by the track was sown to grass, just then growing freshly green. At the northern side, away from the town, trees stood in dense thickets with brush among them like a hedge to confine the backstretch. More trees, not so closely set, contained the two smooth arcs of the turns.

"It is as near an exact mile as measurement can make it," Booth told them.

"How old a course is it, sir?" asked Thane.

"Twenty years," said Booth. "We raced at Williamsburg ever since I can remember, but the old course was a straightaway for quarter-racing."

Thane rode out upon the course and dismounted. He held Penny's reins with one hand while he stooped and felt the earth of the track with the other.

"Loam covered," he reported, "and packed so that it is firm but not hard. It will suit the hoofs of a racing horse."

Nick sat his own saddle and measured the width of the track with his eye. It looked about eighty feet across—enough room for a respectable field of horses, and plenty of space for Janus and Valiant to maneuver when they met.

"Let's go once around, slowly," Thane suggested as he swung astride Penny again.

They made a circuit of the course at an easy amble, Thane ahead and Booth and Nick side by side just behind him. Thane kept his eyes fixed on the track. Several times he reined Penny this way or that. When they came back to the three tall posts, he nodded and smiled in his inverted way.

"I've seen no track as good as this in the colonies north or south," he said authoritatively. "Indeed, I'd say 'twould do credit to an English race meeting—smooth and level as a floor throughout. A mile run here, or four miles, would be as fast as a horse might hope to perform. Janus will outshine himself."

"The same may be said for Valiant," suggested Booth. "He too will outshine himself here."

"Outshine himself, you may be sure, but never will he outshine Janus," said Nick confidently, and Booth smiled at him.

"We'll ride back to our quarters in that spirit," he said. "Saul will give us a good dinner, and afterward we'll see Janus return to his work."

Janus was more than eager to run that afternoon. His hoofs flew in a rattle of speed, and he fairly shot past Circe when she did her best. Thane praised him expertly.

"His greatest need is thoughtful riding," said Thane. "I do begin to think that he understands a race is planned for him. If I should give him his head, he'd rush away at his top speed, whether a horse ran with him or not. He would not check until he fell from simple exhaustion."

" 'A full-tot horse, who being allowed his way—,' " Nick began to quote.

" 'Self-mettle tires him,' " Booth finished the quotation and chuckled when Nick stared. "What, youngster, do you think you're the only one who ever conned Shakespeare? It's from Henry the Eighth, that passage. It shows that Shakespeare understood a horse like Janus, as he understood most matters."

"Shakespeare," repeated Thane weightily. "Ha, I knew a horse of that name once. He had a fine, ground-eating stride as I remember, but he would never have won the day against our Janus. For Janus runs with short steps and can make three of them to one of Shakespeare's."

That remark brought the conversation back to racing.

The General Assembly was sitting in Williamsburg, and many of the members slipped away from a session now and then to come out to the apple farm and watch Janus run. They applauded him loudly. Several offered to wager on Janus, asking no odds. But there were others who had visited Byrd's Westover plantation, and they said that Valiant showed rare form under the conditioning program of Robert Page and Daniel Lewis. Such upholders of Valiant were quick to accept the offered bets of the Janus enthusiasts.

One afternoon at the end of the week, Janus was performing on the track, with Thane carefully training him to respond to a slight check on the reins. Several mounted watchers were there, and Nick sat Circe among them. He heard hoofs approaching behind him and turned in his saddle to see a tall rider in blue on a huge white horse.

"It's young Mr. Forrest, I believe," said a voice he remembered.

"Colonel Washington," Nick greeted him. "Welcome, sir. What brings you to Williamsburg?"

The young colonel halted his horse beside Nick and doffed his cocked hat.

"My duty's at Fort Loudon, to the west among forests and rocks," he replied. "I command that and four other forts, with three hundred and fifty soldiers in their garrisons. We watch for any threat of those Indians the French seek to stir against us. Three hundred and fifty soldiers must be fed and equipped and paid. I am come hither to ask the Assembly to see to those things. Your horse Janus is much in the town's talk, and this morning I thought I'd pay him a visit, as I intend to visit Colonel Booth's Valiant on my way back to the frontier."

Janus cantered by just then, and Washington watched him. "He has a short stride but a swift one," he said. "He covers ground."

"You saw Janus last summer, when he was newly arrived from England," reminded Nick.

"Aye," Washington agreed. "I remember that day, for I had something unpleasant to say to one Captain Magworth."

Nick told him briefly of Magworth's appearance under an assumed name at the Christmas ball at Belleville. Washington's wide mouth grew grim as he listened.

"I've heard that Magworth still dares to venture among the nearby colonies," he said. "They say that he supports himself by gambling and swindling. You seem to have made him your enemy. Beware of Magworth, for he can be violent as well as deceitful."

Booth rode toward them on Dragoon.

"Give you good day, Colonel Washington," he called out. "There are golden reports abroad of your line of defenses against the Indians. I venture to hope that those savages will give you no great trouble."

"I venture to hope so, too," said Washington. "I've learned something of how they can fight, and I count myself lucky to have survived the lesson."

Nick guessed that Washington meant the disastrous Braddock campaign, but did not say so.

Booth held out a book, bound in a soft brown-paper cover. "Here's a diverting thing, just come to my hand from the North," he said. *"Poor Richard's Almanac* 'tis called and is written and published by Mr. Franklin of Philadelphia."

"I've met Mr. Franklin," Washington said, and Nick remembered that Benjamin Franklin, too, had assisted Braddock by gathering supply wagons.

Clamping Dragoon's reins in his bended elbow, Booth opened the almanac. "Now, this is a shrewd maxim," he remarked, and read aloud: " 'Experience keeps a dear school, but fools will learn in no other.' "

Washington's strong features relaxed in a smile. "Mr. Franklin may well say that," he observed. "I was there when he sought to warn General Braddock of danger from the Indians. The general was a brave man, but he had no gift of listening to advice. He believed the Indians might dismay our militia, but they would avail nothing against his British regulars. And, gentlemen, you know what happened to him and to many of his unhappy soldiers."

Again they gave their attention to the performance of Janus. Thane lifted his arm toward Nick in a beckoning gesture. Nick rode out on Circe to pace along with Janus, but Washington's warning about Magworth kept ringing in his ears.

April ended and May began. The odds on the race began to favor Janus against Valiant, five to four. Janus was exercised very carefully indeed, for Nick felt that he was trained to a hair. Mornings and afternoons continued to bring parties of visitors. All were impressed with the way Thane rode. Not even the horsemanship of Daniel Lewis compared to it, they said.

"It's you they are backing, Mr. Thane," said Nick as they sat at supper one evening. "Lucky was our day when we persuaded you to ride for us in this race."

"The finest rider can never win without the best of horses," was Thane's modest reply as he carefully cut away all fat from a slice of boiled beef.

"Yet a poor rider may cause a good horse to run poorly," Booth chimed in. "In town, some say the odds may go to three against two, with Janus favored. A day ago I made the last bet I'll make. One hundred pounds sterling on Janus, against eighty—half in your name, Nick, and half in Mr. Thane's. If we win, you two may divide eighty pounds; and win we shall."

One hundred pounds sterling was worth a hundred and forty pounds Virginia currency, Nick computed quickly. And forty pounds sterling was a tidy sum, enough to pay all his expenses at the College for a year. But Thane greeted this news with one of his taut, upside-down smiles.

"I myself have wagered something on Janus, though they say it's the worst of luck for a rider to back himself," he said. "That shows how speedily I think Janus will carry the odds as favorite."

On Friday, May 6, the day before the race, Booth told Nick that Mrs. Armistead had arrived in Williamsburg, bringing Nancy with her. Thousands of people thronged the streets, and every tavern and lodging house was filled. But Mrs. Armistead had knocked at the door of her old friends, the Greenhows, and had received an instant welcome and hospitality. She had already wagered a hundred pistoles on Janus, at three to two.

That night there was high celebration by some gentlemen at the

Raleigh Tavern. Booth left Saul in charge of the house and stables
while he and Nick and Thane went into town to take part in this
festivity. They rode in as the last twilight faded. Grooms led their
horses to the stable behind the tavern. The public room was gay and
thronged. Mr. Alexander Finnie greeted Booth respectfully and led
him to a private room beyond.

There were tables set with candlesticks and dishes. A merry
company of gentlemen had gathered who wore fine coats, buckled
shoes or shiny boots, and powdered wigs. From long clay pipes rose
clouds of smoke, which seemed to quiver with the chatter and
laughter. There was a gigantic bowl of punch and many bottles of
wine and cider. Hands stretched out on all sides to bid Booth
welcome.

Nick knew that Colonel Washington stopped at the Raleigh when
in town, and he looked around, but did not see him. Robert Page
came through the gathering to speak to Booth and Nick.

"We arrived from Westover last night," said Page, "and hoped
you would be here. Let me make you acquainted with Mr. Daniel
Lewis."

A ready-looking little man of about thirty-five bowed to them.
His queued hair was gingery brown, and he looked as lean and
hard as Thane.

"I know Mr. Lewis, and I am happy to see him again," said
Booth, shaking hands. "Mr. Lewis, this is my young friend and
godson Mr. Nicholas Forrest, who has done much toward training
Janus. And here also is Mr. Carr Thane, whom you'll see again
tomorrow, when he will be on the back of Janus."

Thane held out his gaunt hand, and Lewis shook it.

"Sir, your most humble servant," Lewis said. "They predict we'll
have fair weather for that little run of ours tomorrow."

"I expect we shall," replied Thane, "for a shoulder blade I
cracked once in a fall usually aches when rain is coming."

"What, sir, you say you once fell from a horse?" inquired Page.

"Let me hear someone say he never fell from a horse, and I know
he never mounted one," replied Thane gravely. "In any event, my
shoulder is without pain tonight. May the best horse win, is my
hope."

"Don't tell me you already concede to Valiant!" Page laughed.

"If I can guess Thane's mind, Janus was in it when he spoke," said Booth. "But our dinner is about to be served. Let's sit like true friends and enjoy it together."

It was a very fine dinner indeed, with wine to go with it. Toasts were called for here and there. Page rose to propose the health of Valiant, and Booth responded by drinking to Janus. Nick saw that Lewis drank only part of a single glass of wine. As for Thane, he no more than touched his lips to his when a toast was proclaimed. At length, Lewis excused himself, saying that he wanted a good night's rest. Thane rose with him. They went out together, talking like friends.

The rest of the company continued to eat, drink, laugh and joke, but Nick stirred in his chair.

"Your pardon, Mr. Booth, and yours, Mr. Page," he said. "Maybe I'd be wise to go, too."

"Aye, growing boys need their hours of sleep," said Page cheerfully.

"Call Nick a boy if you will, but he has played the man in getting Janus ready," said Booth. "Go you on, Nick, and I myself won't stay long. All of us will do well to be bright-eyed tomorrow."

Nick bowed himself away from the table, left the noisy club room, and headed out at the front door. "Shall I send for your horse to be brought, sir?" asked a servant.

"I know where the stables are," said Nick. "I'll go get her myself."

He made haste around to the side and then to the back of the tavern building. Two horses stood there in the dark, with two men holding them. So earnestly did these two men talk that they did not notice Nick as he moved past and into the open stable.

But then a voice spoke, and Nick knew that voice as he had known the voice of Washington.

"It's agreed then, Thane?"

Captain Magworth was speaking, out there by the horses. Nick stood motionless to listen.

"Quite agreed," Thane answered, "but for the payment. I want half the money now, or tomorrow Janus shall win, as best I can make him."

XI

Struggle in the Night

Nick stood as motionless as a fence post, just inside the jamb of the open door. He held his breath to listen.

"Stay," Magworth was saying. "A groom or scullion walked past us just now and went into those stables. How's your Latin, Thane?"

"I have no Latin," Nick heard Thane reply.

"French, then. It's an unfashionable language these days of war. Know you what *'cheval'* means?"

"Aye, that much French I know," Thane said. "I've talked it now and then, with Frenchmen in London."

"Hark then, and carefully: *Il faut que votre cheval non fait le cours. Comprenez?*"

Magworth's French was not very good, but understandable. Nick blessed fate for those studies to which Booth had set him.

"Lentement, lentement," Thane was telling Magworth. "Slowly. *Mot à mot."*

He wanted Magworth to speak a word at a time, and Magworth did so: *"Votre—cheval—non—fait—le—cours—."*

Your horse must not make the race, that meant. Janus must not race. This time, Thane understood.

"Ah, oui," he agreed. *"C'est entendu."* Then, in English again, "How are we to manage?"

*"Avec un—*blast me, what's the word?*—avec un canif au jarret."*

Canif meant knife. *Jarret* meant the hock, the joint of a horse's

86

hind leg. *Canif au jarret,* in Magworth's slipshod French, meant that Janus was to be hamstrung. Nick felt himself grow cold to the very tips of his fingers and toes.

"Oui," said Thane again. "Next, Captain, the finances. Half the money now."

"Le demi d'un mille des livres," agreed Magworth. He would give half of a thousand pounds.

"In gold," Thane insisted.

"Je n'ai pas ces monnaies en or," Magworth protested. *"Bilets de banc, en papier."*

He was offering bank notes, then.

"C'est bien," Thane said, with an air of making a concession. *"Donnez-moi."*

Nick stood so breathlessly still that he could hear the faint crackling of paper as Magworth paid the notes into Thane's hand.

"And the other half as soon as it's done," said Magworth briskly, returning to English. "Let's up and away."

Nick heard their saddles creak as they mounted. The horses stamped the ground as they left. The power of motion returned to Nick.

While Magworth and Thane had talked of how they would cripple Janus, Nick could not have stirred or spoken. Bitterly he blamed himself for not rushing out and denouncing them. Now he stole into the dark stable, his hand on the wall to guide him. Deep within the long building hung a light. It showed him a row of stalls, with the heads of horses thrusting out above the low doors. He ran to where Circe peered at him.

"Swiftly, girl, we're in sore trouble," he told her softly. "And Janus is in peril."

Her saddle was set on a nearby rack, with her bridle across it. Nick seized the bridle and coaxed the bit into her mouth. He fastened the throat latch under her jowl and led her out. With no thought of taking time to saddle her, he flung the reins over her head and leaped mightily to throw himself astride of her bare back.

"Hi!" he shouted, and drummed her flanks with his heels. Out of the stable he rode, and around the side of the tavern. At the very edge of the street he reined Circe to a halt. He leaned to shout at the staring servant outside the big front door.

"Two riders," Nick called. "Just now they came from the stables. Which way have they gone?"

The fellow gaped at him in the light of the lamps. "Young sir, your saddle—"

"I'm riding tonight without one," Nick shouted him down. "Which way have they gone, I say?"

The servant waved a shaky arm eastward. That direction would take Magworth and Thane to Waller Street, and beyond that to the country road to the apple farm.

Still Nick held Circe and addressed the servant. "Hark you, go in and inquire for Mr. Mordecai Booth," he said. "Tell him, a message from Nicholas Forrest. There is dire danger to his horse Janus."

"But—" the servant quavered.

"A matter of life and death, tell him!" roared Nick, and waited no longer. He whacked Circe smartly on the shoulder and was out on the street going eastward.

Somebody's carriage rolled toward him, almost in the center of the street. It was set with lamps right and left, and was drawn by two trotting horses with arched necks. Nick reined Circe to the very edge of the street to escape a collision. More traffic appeared along the street as he hurried Circe past the carriage, but he could see no

pair of horsemen riding toward the east. Magworth and Thane must be well ahead of him.

Just past the Capitol, a road branched off northward, toward Capitol Landing above. It was a direct route to the apple farm, and Nick reined left to take it. There was only a scrap of moon to give him light, but he put Circe to the half-seen road and she galloped boldly upon it.

Around a tree-bordered curve of the way they went. Around another. Minutes were passing, and to Nick they seemed like ages. He leaned above Circe's flying mane to make out the house among the orchard trees. Lights showed in the windows. Closer he rode, and he could see two horses standing in front. Magworth and Thane had dismounted there.

He dared not ride close, lest Circe's hoofbeats give them warning. He reined her to a slower pace and flung himself from her bare back. His feet struck the turf at the side of the road. For a moment he half floundered to keep from falling. Then he got his balance and sprinted in among the trees. Low he crouched, to avoid striking the branches. He headed for the rear yard where the stable stood.

As at the Raleigh Tavern, the stable door stood open and the rays of a lighted lantern came softly through. Nick gained the edge of the orchard and stopped, panting with the strain of his frantic sprint. He looked toward the stable door.

Two figures stood there, looking down at a third figure that lay prone and motionless upon the threshold. Nick stole toward them in the night.

"Ha, he kept a sleepy watch here," Magworth's voice exulted. "He never knew I was upon him until I struck from behind."

Closer Nick moved, on the tips of his toes. It was Saul who lay there, limp, silent. Nick felt his teeth grit together in deadly fury.

Thane's smaller body stooped. "Is he dead?"

"No, he breathes," said Magworth. "My pistol butt knocked his wits out of his head, that's all. He won't move for minutes yet. Go in, Thane, and do your appointed work on that Janus horse."

Thane straightened again. He looked into the stable and seemed to hesitate. Nick, creeping nearer across the grass, fought to keep from breathing audibly.

"Go, I say," Magworth urged. "Earn your money. I've struck down this stableman, and that's enough for me this night. And you know best where the tendon is, and how quickest to slice it through."

Thane rummaged a pocket and brought something out. In the light from the door, it was recognizable—a big clasp knife. There was a snick like the drawing back of a hammer on a gun as Thane opened out the blade.

"Put up that knife, you scoundrelly skulk!" yelled Nick with what breath he had, and charged at them.

Both turned at his cry. Magworth poised a big horse pistol in his hand, Thane held the open knife.

"Sink me, it's that mouthy boy of Booth's," Magworth growled. "We'll have to finish him."

"And with no noise," said Thane bleakly. "Leave him to me."

He faced Nick, his booted feet wide apart, his lean shoulders hunched. The knife lifted in his right hand. He extended his left as though to paw toward Nick. The blade caught a wink of light. It looked long and cruel.

But Nick took no time to be afraid of that sharp steel. He flung himself at Thane. The knife licked out at him like a striking snake, but Nick seized and clamped Thane's wrist with his own left hand. His right fist struck with all his sinewy young weight behind it. He smashed Thane full on the mouth, and Thane's head snapped back. His hat flew off and fell to the ground beside the quiet form of Saul. Next instant Nick grappled him, still pinning the knife wrist, and tried to lift and throw him.

Thane was smaller than Nick, but he seemed made of iron. He kept his feet and tried to clutch Nick by the throat with his left hand. Together they strained and stumbled this way and that.

"Pull clear of him, Thane!" Magworth was crying.

Over Thane's shoulder, Nick saw Magworth draw himself up tall. He leveled the big pistol.

"Pull clear of him!" roared Magworth again. "Give me a chance at him with a bullet!"

Those loud cries seemed to bring Saul back to life. As Nick wrestled with Thane, he saw Saul rise groggily on hands and knees. Then Saul flung himself forward, whipping his strong arms around Magworth's booted legs. Magworth yelled a curse into the night as he lost his footing and fell heavily. As he struck the ground, the pistol spun out of his hand and through the open stable door.

Nick paid him no more attention, but got his right hand up, with its heel against Thane's face. He put all his strength into a powerful shove that sent Thane staggering free. Again Nick struck, and his knuckles came solidly home on the point of Thane's jaw. Once more Nick planted a blow. As Thane reeled before it, Nick shot out a foot and tripped him. Thane, too, went down.

Nick leaped over Thane's falling body and ran toward the door where the lantern light showed him the fallen pistol. Magworth had kicked and struggled free of Saul's tackling grip. He scrambled on all fours after the weapon, but Nick got there first. He bent and snatched the pistol from the ground and leaped clear of Magworth's pawing hand.

Circe came trotting past them, to seek her stall. Nick paid no attention to her.

"Don't make a false move, Captain," cautioned Nick, sliding his finger through the trigger guard and drawing back the hammer with his thumb. "No false move, I say, or 'twill be your last in a life of false moves."

Magworth rose to his knees. Thane got up, his knife still in his hand. Saul, too, slowly found his feet.

"That pistol isn't loaded," Magworth muttered, but Nick laughed down at him.

"That's a lie, and it won't help you," Nick taunted. "A moment ago you were telling Thane to stand clear, that you might put a bullet into me. Nay, stay on your knees, you look better that way." He spared Thane a glance. "And you, sir, drop that knife. Quick's the word."

He pointed the pistol. Thane let the knife go. As it struck the ground, Saul grabbed it and straightened again. Saul was still unsteady on his feet, and blood flowed from a cut on his scalp, but the knife in his hand seemed to give him strength.

"Things getting different, Master Nick," he said. "They knocked me down when I wasn't looking. Now I'm looking. Let them try me again if they dare."

"And so," Nick said, looking from Magworth to Thane and back. "And so you were going to cripple Janus."

"Nay, no such thing—," began Magworth.

"Yet again you seek to lie," Nick cut him off. "I heard you when you spoke there behind the Raleigh Tavern. 'Twas in French, and sorry French at that, but I heard and understood. Mr. Thane, you haven't earned that blood money he gave you."

"I fell in with him because I was afraid," Thane tried to plead. "He's head of a ring of gamblers with all their money wagered on Valiant."

"Don't listen to him," said Magworth, rocking from one knee to the other. "It was his own plot to line his pockets. He came to us with the plan. I should never have entertained the thought."

"There at least you speak truth," Nick nodded above the pistol. He felt like a judge on the bench with convicted criminals before him. "Whoever thought of this cruel deed against a poor harmless horse, you're both in it together."

A noise of hoofs on the road, in the yard. Then booted feet rushing.

"Nick!" Booth shouted. "What was that warning you sent? Who are these others?"

He hurried and puffed to where the light from the stable showed his concerned face. At his elbow was Nelson.

"You said something had befallen Janus," he said.

"I have not been to him, but I pray heaven he was not harmed," Nick replied. "Thane here took money from Captain Magworth and agreed to hamstring Janus. I got here just as they struck Saul down and Thane drew his knife."

"It's the truth," Saul assured the newcomers. "Let me make sure that Janus is all right."

Still carrying the knife, he hurried into the stable. At last Magworth got slowly to his feet. Booth had a pistol, too, as big as the one Nick had captured. He held it ready as he confronted Magworth.

"Put up your guns, I pray you," said Magworth, in a voice that suddenly sounded weak and sick. "Nay, I surrender. I'll go with you like a lamb. My evil star was in the sky tonight."

He moved slowly and stood beside Thane. Nelson came toward them, as if to stand guard.

Saul came back out of the stable. Blood smeared his brow, but he smiled.

"Janus is all right, Master Booth," he announced happily. "He is asleep in his stall, and not a hair on his body harmed."

"Happy am I to hear it," Booth replied. "Now, to the house with these rogues. More of my friends are on their way here from town, and officers among them. They'll put this unhappy pair in Williamsburg jail." He clapped Nick on the shoulder. "If Janus has no hurt, all will be well when we race him tomorrow."

"But who will ride Janus, sir?" Nick asked.

"Who will ride Janus?" Booth said after him. "Why, who but you, lad?"

XII

The Day of the Race

The events of the rest of the night seemed blurred to Nick, almost like a dream.

Brought back to the house, Magworth and Thane made sullen confessions of the whole plot. A band of gamblers had pooled all their resources to back Valiant, then feared loss of their money because of the word that Thane rode so brilliantly. When Magworth had tried to bribe Thane, the thought of keeping Janus to a slow pace was too much for Thane's vanity. He did not want to be the losing rider. He said he would hamstring Janus, to make Valiant the winner by default, for a thousand pounds sterling.

Nick had arrived just as Magworth struck Saul from behind and stunned him. A matter of a few moments more would have seen Janus forever disabled. The deed done, as Thane confessed, the alarm would have been raised. Thane would have said that he had arrived as the plotters fled, and would have given false descriptions of them.

Magworth named his partners in the gambling ring, and Booth grimly wrote them down. Among them were several of the most unsavory rascals in all Virginia. When more men came from Williamsburg to lead the prisoners away, they promised to arrest Magworth's friends.

Both Nick and Saul said they would keep guard over Janus every moment until race time. They dragged cots to the stable. Nick lay

95

down, but stayed awake, wide-eyed, and troubled in the darkness.

He, who never had taken part in any important race, must ride Janus on the morrow. And he had not sat on Janus' back for many weeks. True, he and Janus had always loved and understood each other. Tossing on the cot, Nick reflected that being on terms of understanding friendship with any horse was a rare thing. True, horses knew what you said, but they did not always try to say things themselves. Their signals were slight ones, a crinkling of the muzzle or a flick of the ear, sometimes a whinny, a nudge with the nose. They did not strive to make their thoughts known, as dogs do, when the human companion did not seem ready to comprehend. If Nick and Janus understood each other and told each other things, it was a truly unusual relationship.

Against them would race William Byrd's Valiant, years younger than Janus, proud and swift and confident. He had a skillful, experienced rider, who knew Valiant well. Daniel Lewis had been a famous gentleman jockey for years. Nick was a lad in his teens, wise perhaps for his years, but with much, much more to learn.

"All I can do is my best," he muttered, half aloud. "That is all anyone can do, in any stern trial."

At last he slept, soundly and dreamlessly, until Saul tapped his shoulder to waken him in the dawn.

Nick hurried at once to where Janus, too, was waking. Janus recognized him with a low whinny, almost as soft as the purr of a cat.

"Know you that this is the day?" Nick asked him, stroking his neck. "The two of us must do our utmost. I'll ride you, Janus. Do you know what I say?"

Janus butted his nose against Nick's shoulder, as though to say that he understood very well.

Nick went outside, to look at the sky. It was cloudless and blue, and the air had the soft, bright warmth of spring. Saul came and stood with him, a strip of white bandage on his wounded head.

"Are you nervous, Master Nick?" Saul asked.

"Nay, I can't be nervous," replied Nick at once. "If a rider is nervous, his horse knows it."

"You talk like one who's going to play the man today," said Saul. "Come, breakfast is ready at the house."

Nick had only a cup of coffee, a small piece of dry toast and one boiled egg. Mordecai Booth ate swiftly and heartily. He made an end of his meal and stood up.

"I make haste to ride into town," he said. "Starting time is two of the clock. Be there at noon, you and Saul. I'll be next the judges' stand, and I'll have all ready to tend Janus."

He clutched Nick's lean hand in his broad one and looked searchingly into Nick's eyes.

"Lad, you know what this race means to me, to us all," he said earnestly. "'Tis not only a question of money wagered or fame to be won, not even of rivalry with my friend Byrd. Racing is in our blood, as it flows in the blood of fine horses."

"That's true, sir," agreed Nick solemnly.

"By heaven, I wonder how many thousands of years good men have felt their hearts rise to see swift, brave horses run against each other," mused Booth. "Horses can example the best of men, Nick. Often I ask if here's not one of the great instances of high courage —horses bred to run and strive for first place, to delight all who love and praise strong, true hearts."

With that, he strode out. Nick and Saul went back to the stable. Again they looked at Janus, and Janus looked thoughtfully back at them.

"At least he's in the finest condition to which we could bring him," said Nick. "See his coat, how it shines like satin. And how hard and ready his muscles lie beneath. Who'd think he was eleven years old?"

"How do you aim to ride him, Master Nick?" Saul asked.

"I hope I won't keep him from his own wish and effort," Nick answered. "Mayhap 'twill be best to get ahead from the very tap of the drum. After that, a speed to outrun Valiant, but never such a speed as will tire him."

"That for the first heat?" suggested Saul. "Then what?"

"Nay, I cannot think beyond those first four miles," Nick said.

When it was time to dress, Nick donned a thin shirt and linen riding breeches. He chose his lightest boots, drew them on, and buckled blunted prick spurs to the heels.

An hour before noon they set out. Nick rode Circe and led Janus, who was draped in his cloaklike cloth. Saul sat on Penny and held

the halter of the wagon horse that bore things they would need. Into Williamsburg they rode, and at the very edge of town throngs of people gathered, heading for the race track. Many of them hailed Janus.

"Good luck to the brave horse!" Nick heard a shout, and others joined in a chorus of encouragement.

Even so early, the whole circuit of the track was edged with knots and groups of spectators. Some sat in the branches of the trees. More arrived with every passing second. A number had brought baskets of food and sat on the grass to eat bread and meat and to drink from wine bottles and beer jugs. They made way for Nick and Janus to come to where Booth waited at the right of the three poles that marked the starting point. Great red streamers fluttered from those posts.

Booth greeted Nick eagerly as he dismounted.

"Here's Mr. Nelson, who insists on making one of our party," said Booth. "Aye, and behind us is Mrs. Armistead, who could not be kept away."

"Not all the Virginia regiments could hold me from this race," cried Mrs. Armistead. She stood, parasol on high, beside her carriage. "Son-in-law, you will remember what I vowed last summer. Your Janus must win today, to repay my efforts and expenses on behalf of you and Belleville plantation."

"I could not help remembering, ma'am, what with your remindings," Booth said to her. "Nick, by now all Williamsburg knows the tale of how Thane sought to betray us and cripple Janus, and that you are riding in his stead. The odds have changed again. They are seven to five on Valiant."

"Valiant," repeated Nick, and looked beyond the three poles to where the rival headquarters had been set up.

For the first time he saw the tall, proud horse against which he must ride Janus. Valiant towered among his attendants, clean-limbed and high-headed. He was dun-colored, a hint of gray in the brown. Page and Lewis stood talking to two grooms.

Saul was with Janus, washing out his mouth with a dripping sponge. Booth stooped above an open satchel and brought out a jacket of light-blue silk.

"'Twas made to Thane's measure," he said, holding it for Nick to put on. "You and he are almost of a size."

Nick buttoned the jacket from belt to throat. It was snug upon his chest and shoulders, but it did not cramp him. Booth gave him a blue cap with a leather visor.

"Nick," said a soft voice at his elbow.

He swung around to face Nancy Tyll. She wore blue muslin, with a broad-brimmed straw hat set upon her dark hair and tied beneath her chin with a bow of light blue ribbon.

"I must wish you good fortune," she said.

"And for that I do thank you, Nancy," replied Nick. "I hope you wear that ribbon because it is the color for which Janus races today."

"I wear it for Janus, and for his rider," she said, gazing at Nick's jacket that matched the ribbon. "I heard with admiration of your sense and high courage, shown last night. Sense and courage will help you win today."

"Ha, think you I'll win?"

"I'm certain of it," she said. "And I have wagered on you."

Nick gazed at her, goggle-eyed, and she smiled.

"When Cousin Armistead heard that odds were against Janus, seven to five, she hurried with all her money to back him," Nancy said. "And I had five golden pistoles. I gave it to her, and asked her to wager it for me."

She held out her hand to Nick, and he took it, wonderingly. Then she smiled again and went back to Mrs. Armistead's carriage.

Nick watched the tending of Janus, his heart beating fast. Saul stooped his bandaged head as he rubbed the clean-muscled brown legs. Nick helped strip away the cloth and brought the saddle cloth and saddle. Carefully Nick adjusted the girth to clasp but not to squeeze the powerful body. When Saul brought the bridle, Janus opened his mouth readily for the bit.

"He wants to run," said Saul. "Run faster than Valiant."

The track was thronged by now, all around its outer and inner edges. Watchers sat on their horses or in their carriages or stood shoulder to shoulder. There was a loud din of many voices. But Janus was calm.

Booth and Page met the judges at the stand. Nick watched the toss of a coin to decide position. Booth hurried back to say that he had won the toss.

"Put him close on the inner hand at the line," he ordered Nick.

A bugle sounded warning. All stood away as Nick set foot in stirrup, swung his leg over the saddle, and picked up the reins. He rode to where a line had been drawn in the earth of the track, and brought Janus to position just opposite the three poles. Valiant walked springily across. Lewis was clad in a dark-blue jacket and a dark-blue cap, with facings of red like those on the uniform of the Virginia infantry. Lewis reined Valiant into place some forty feet to the right of Janus. Saul stood beside Janus, his hand holding the bridle close to the bit.

"Ready?" a judge called to Nick. "Are you ready?"

"Aye," said Nick, his mouth suddenly as dry as cinders.

A sudden silence fell. All the world seemed to hold its breath. Then the thump of the drum.

Janus was off like an arrow from the bow, in a new concerted roar from all those regiments of spectators.

The posts rushed backward at Nick's left, almost within touch of Janus' flank. Nick leaned well forward, reins almost free, his feet toed in to keep the spurs from touching Janus. He spared one glance to see Valiant in a swift slant across in an effort to capture the lead. He shook the reins a trifle, and Janus picked up speed. More yells as Janus reached the beginning of the first turn and scuttled around. Valiant was close behind.

"Ha, Janus! Janus!" watchers were shouting on both sides of the track. Janus seemed to hear, and he increased his speed. Yells all along the way as they went around the turn, Valiant thundering after, and into the backstretch.

The trees were full of onlookers, between the trunks and up in the forked branches. They screamed wildly. Nick kept Janus to the track's inner border, posts flashing away in a procession. Valiant was exerting himself with long, swift strides. His head crept up. His nose came opposite Janus' flank. But then they reached the second turn, and Nick made Janus hug it closely for the advantage of the inner way. Valiant dropped back despite himself.

On the forward stretch, Janus scrambled nobly. To Nick it seemed that the two horses were like beetles, rushing frantically around the rim of a gigantic platter. The three poles and the judges flashed past and away to the rear. Nick had not time to see where Booth and Saul and the others stood. On he forged toward the turn, a length ahead.

The second mile went the same way, a headlong gallop with Janus leading, and the third mile saw him keep that lead. Bending down, Nick snatched a glance under his own arm as they reached the turn of the final mile. Lewis, too, leaned forward and plied the whip in his right hand, on this side and the other.

"On, on!" Nick urged Janus in the backstretch. He slackened the reins to give Janus his head for full speed. Up came the second turn, and around they went as though whirled at the end of a cable.

Then the homestretch, and from both sides a mass of leaning heads, a tossing forest of lifted arms. The noise of the cheering seemed to shake the earth and the sky.

"Faster!" Nick besought Janus, who heard the cry and knew what it meant. Janus seemed to cleave the air as a fish cleaves water.

There came the three poles with their streamers, and among them the judges with watches in their hands. And a final deafening howl on all sides, "JANUS TAKES THE FIRST HEAT!"

Nick reined him to a canter, brought him around, and headed him back. Spectators waved, shouted, and jumped up and down. Valiant was making a turn, too, coming back to his place.

Nick was suddenly aware of the great heaving rise and fall of Janus' sides as he gulped for air.

XIII

The Heroic Distance

Mordecai Booth rushed to catch Janus by the bridle and lead him to where the others waited to begin their ministrations. Nick dropped to earth and began to loosen the cinch. Booth had flung off his coat and rolled up his sleeves. In his right hand, he clutched a sweat knife. With it he began to scrape the lathery perspiration from the heaving chestnut flanks of Janus.

Nick, too, panted as though he had run that four miles on his own feet. Nancy Tyll came close, holding out a stone jug.

"Coffee," she said. "Still hot, I think. Take some, it will give you strength."

Gratefully Nick lifted the jug and took a mouthful of the hot, strong brew. But he did not swallow more than a trickle. He swirled the liquid in his mouth and kept it there. Pulling off the visored cap, he mopped his brow with his gold-hooped sleeve. The day seemed oppressively hot, hotter than midsummer.

"Say not a word," Nancy said. "Save your every breath for the race. Nick, you rode wonderfully."

He spat out the coffee. "Janus ran wonderfully," he gurgled.

"I told you, say nothing."

Saul dipped a sponge in a bucket. Mrs. Armistead bustled up and took the sponge from him.

"Let me," she said and carefully washed out Janus' mouth. Then she held up something in her other hand. It was wet and red.

103

"'Tis a morsel of bread, soaked in the best port wine," she said and held it out to Janus on her palm.

His lips stretched to take the fragment. Saul had snatched up a wad of dry straw. He squatted to rub the quivering forelegs.

"Poor Janus, he labors for breath," Nick muttered.

"So does Valiant yonder," William Nelson said, pointing toward where the great dun horse stood among his host of handlers.

Nick saw, and felt hope flare up within him. Daniel Lewis had fairly poured the whip onto Valiant, in his effort to take that first heat, but he had whipped Valiant in vain. Meanwhile, what half an hour's respite could do for Janus would be done. He stood and watched Booth and Saul and Nelson rub Janus all over with straw and dry cloths, then with other cloths dipped in warm water. Nick walked close to Janus and gazed into his eyes. They were still brilliant, those eyes.

"Well done," said Nick. "But we still have it to do."

Janus made no sound, but his lips fluttered as though in reply. Nick touched him gently on the cheek. He knew joy and determination, and with it an impulse to shed a tear or two.

Four miles—the heroic distance. It had seemed to tax Nick's own strength and determination, and he had only ridden. What of Janus, eleven years old and fourteen hands high, running against Valiant's long legs and defiant youth? Nick wished desperately that he himself weighed nothing, that he was no bigger than a cat or a monkey, to lighten the burden for Janus.

Booth came to his shoulder. "Nick, we'd best get the saddle on," he said. "The second heat will be called within minutes."

"Janus must win again," said Nick.

"I pray he will, but if Valiant wins, there's a third heat to decide the race."

"Janus must win this second heat," Nick said again. "He might not win a third. True, he would run his short-legged best against that mighty stride, but if Valiant wins now, he is most apt to win again."

"Valiant must not win," Mrs. Armistead told them sharply.

"See how Janus breathes and gasps," said Nick. "Valiant is weary, too, but Valiant is younger. It's like a young man fighting an old one. The old fighter must win ere he fails and faints."

William Nelson joined them. "Take this," he said, holding out a riding crop, but Nick waved it away.

"Never the whip," he said, and turned to look Janus in the eyes again. "Never a whip in my hand for you, boy," he promised. "You'll run to your last step and your last breath without it. That much I know."

The eyes looked back. They seemed to understand him, to make a promise of a stark, last-ditch battle. Janus was standing strongly again. His chestnut sides did not labor like a bellows any more.

"How does his right shoulder seem?" Nick asked Saul.

"As far as I can judge, it's sound, Master Nick. I hope we'll win."

"We must win," Mrs. Armistead cried at them. Her old eyes snapped, her bonnet tossed like a ship on a stormy sea.

A bugle blew its warning note. Nick tested the saddle girth and mounted. Janus moved bravely out upon the track. Myriads of voices were shouting his name.

It was Valiant's turn to start where he chose. Lewis set him where Janus stood before, at the track's inner edge next to the three poles where the judges waited. Nick checked Janus with his front hoofs at the line some thirty feet away and faced him ever so slightly inward.

"Together," Nick whispered to Janus. "We're together—get us there."

Janus quivered, as though his nerves were fiddlestrings drawn tight. He was ready. He wanted to run and to win.

BOOM! The drum spoke, the crowd roared, and Janus and Valiant were off like startled birds.

Midway in his leap, Janus floundered ever so slightly, and Valiant grabbed the lead as Janus had grabbed it in the first heat. Recovering, Janus scurried to catch up. His hoofs sounded like the fall of hail in a storm. Valiant, spurning the ground away behind him, sped to the beginning of the first turn. Janus came close behind, his outstretched nose almost at the toss of Valiant's brown tail. Valiant raced as close as he could to the inside of the track on the turn. Lewis bent forward, he did not look back.

The crowd's hundreds of voices screamed. "Valiant! Valiant!" they were crying. Valiant was ahead. The crowd cheered him, as in

the first heat it had cheered for Janus. Nick hated every soul in that packed mass of loud-mouthed people. He shut them out of hearing, out of sight and mind, and concentrated on keeping his hands and body moving to the rhythm of Janus' rattling pace.

Janus stretched his neck and pushed his head forward. So did Nick, crouching in his saddle until the toss of Janus' mane flicked his face. Ahead of them raced Valiant's powerful dun quarters, and the dark blue of Daniel Lewis' jacket. Up rose Lewis' arm, and down it came. Lewis was whipping Valiant to greater effort.

"Catch him!" Nick pleaded, and Janus tried. They rushed along the backstretch to the second turn and spun around it. The posts crowded near, flying rearward at the left. On into the start of the second mile they raced. Valiant had gained a position half a dozen feet ahead of Janus. All those people along the track seemed to be bellowing encouragement to Valiant.

"Never hark to them, Janus," said Nick earnestly.

Janus pluckily closed the distance as they came to the turn. But Valiant's long legs seemed to grow longer. His hoofs fairly clutched the ground ahead and hurled it under and behind him. Lewis was spurring and whipping. In the backstretch of that second mile, Valiant strove fully twenty feet to the fore. He looked smaller up there ahead, he looked far away.

Nick loosened the bridle and turned his toes out to touch Janus with the spurs. It was only a nudge, an appeal. Janus responded with a swifter drumming of hoofs. He came closer at the turn, shortened the gap as they started the third mile.

"Janus!" someone whooped loudly. Perhaps that had been Booth or Nelson. Up there in front, Lewis plied his whip again. For all Valiant's youth, for all his long, leaping legs, for all that sting of the lash on his flanks, he could not keep his spacious lead. Janus gained. It was a gain of inch by bitter inch, but Janus was wearing his way forward.

"Brave horse!" cried Nick, leaning above the toss of the mane, and nudged the spurs against Janus.

From wherever his proud strength was kept, Janus brought forth an ounce more. Valiant, too, was deserving his name. He did his best, and his best was considerable. But Janus crept upon him. Nearer and ever nearer forged Janus, around the second turn, and toward the start of the fourth mile, that last mile of the heroic distance. As the judges' stand flashed by, Janus had come up to Valiant's fluttering tail once more.

Lewis did not look back at them. Perhaps he did not dare. He sat with knees high and shoulders bent, like a monkey. He seemed as though he was trying to drag Valiant ahead. The crowd yelled, but the yelling sound fogged. Nick had eyes and mind and will only for Valiant up there and for reaching Valiant and passing him.

At the turn, Valiant was running with no pull on the reins. Around he went, close to the inner side—but not as close this time as before, not quite. Nick's dry lips drew back from his set teeth. Could he, could Janus—?

Before he answered that, Janus decided. He thundered close to the poles, closer than Valiant. Up he shoved, his head suddenly inside Valiant's quarter, running, running, and the wind rushing into Nick's face.

At the very center of the turn, Janus made his move. A narrow space showed for an instant, and the space and instant were enough. Janus drove his nose forward, opposite Valiant's flank. If Valiant swerved left, Janus might be dashed against those posts that flew backward. But as the voices of the crowd rose to a shattering screech, and Lewis glanced toward Janus, the thing was done.

They whirled around into the backstretch of the final mile. Janus was on the inside, neck and neck with Valiant.

As in a murky dream, Nick heard Lewis shouting at Valiant and saw that whip flogging. Janus ran so close to the posts that Nick braced himself to feel them brush his boot and hurl it from the stirrup. But it did not happen. Nick bent double against the gale that Janus was running up against them. Neck and neck, girth and girth, Janus and Valiant galloped the backstretch. The hard track sailed away behind them. Up ahead, Nick saw the final turn of that final mile.

"Now, Janus!" he cried, and Janus found within himself one last increase of speed.

They hurtled along the track. The red streamers fluttered up to the left, Valiant rushed at the right. All the voices blared a name, but Nick could not hear it. He flashed past the finish point. The race was over.

He rose high in his stirrups, checking Janus to a slower scamper, to a lope. He brought Janus around. Valiant was coming around, too. Lewis sat up straight, trying to shout something at Nick above all the shouting.

Then a rush of people upon the track and close on all sides. Mordecai Booth, in his shirt sleeves, reached a hand for Janus' bridle. Booth's eyes bulged, his mouth opened. He led Janus with one hand and with the other pushed people out of the way.

Nick still stood up in the stirrups, trying to understand, to know. Then he knew.

Booth was bringing them to the stand where the judges waited. One judge pointed at Janus with his left hand, while his right rose high in the air. All of the cheering before was as nothing to the cheering now.

Janus came to a halt, and Nick felt faint and fuzzy. He took his feet from the stirrups and almost fell to earth. His knees wavered.

"You won by a head only," Booth was gasping in his ear. "But you won!"

"Janus won," Nick said, his tongue dry as an autumn leaf. He staggered forward two steps and flung his arms around the lathered neck of Janus, pressing his face against it.

Men pulled him free again, slapping his back, hugging him, yelling exultant praises.

"'Twas Janus," he kept saying dully. "Janus won, I but rode him."

Daniel Lewis came to shake hands. "At least we ran you up to the eyebrows," Lewis said. "What a ride you gave your horse."

"You're too kind, sir."

"When you dared drive inside at the turn yonder—," Lewis began.

"'Twas not my doing," Nick said. "Janus saw the chance and took it."

Through the tumult he got to where Saul and Mrs. Armistead waited. Mrs. Armistead had flung away her parasol, and her bonnet tossed awry on her head.

"Nobly ridden, Nick!" she squalled. "You rode as I'd have ridden, had I been born a man. And here's Nancy, to compliment you."

Smiling radiantly, Nancy Tyll caught Nick's shoulders in her hands. She hugged him and kissed him strongly. All around them cheered and applauded, as at a play. When Nancy drew back, her cheek was smeared with sweaty grime from Nick's face.

"Here, youngster." It was John Tayloe, holding out a silver cup. "'Tis wine and water, mixed together. Drink it slowly, mind."

As he sipped, Nick watched Janus. Saul wiped the weary, victorious legs and body with straw. Booth shook out the great cloth, ready to drape over him. Nick went and fumbled at the saddle girth.

Robert Page was there, congratulating Booth, while Nelson and Tayloe listened.

"Your Janus is the greatest racer in all America," Page said.

"Amen to that," seconded Tayloe. "Sirs, I'm for all of us subscribing to back him against any horse who dares come against him."

"No," said Booth, spreading out the cloth in his hands.

Nelson stared. "What, man, have you lost your senses?" he demanded. "But with Janus, you'll be the foremost racing man among us all, North or South."

"I do not listen," said Booth. "Janus won today, aye—with almost the last grain of strength in his body. This noble beast shall never run another race."

Nick drew the saddle from Janus' sweaty back and turned to looked happily at Booth.

"Let him live on in his glory," proclaimed Booth. "Let him live and be happy. He shall found a whole nation of racers to carry on his name when all of us have departed this earth."

XIV

George Washington Speaks

General George Washington, commander of all the American armies, pored over papers at his headquarters desk at Morristown in New Jersey. Sleet rattled at the window; February of 1780 was cold, and Washington had just sent an urgent plea to Congress for new, warm overcoats for his soldiers. The aide on duty in the outer room opened the door.

"Major Forrest is here at your bidding, General," he said.

"Let him come in," said Washington, and rose. Years of warfare had lined his strong face and had sprinkled his red hair with gray, but he still kept the sinewy, towering horseman's figure of a quarter century earlier. A lean officer in blue and buff entered and stood at salute. Washington took a long step toward him and held out his big hand.

"Happy I am to see you, my friend," he welcomed Major Nicholas Forrest. "Shut the door, I'll tell you what may stir your blood. Come and we'll sit at the desk together."

Nick, too, had kept a youthful hardness of muscle, though he was almost forty. He sat beside Washington, who handed him a written report.

"We've fought the British well, and I dare feel hopeful of success at the North," said Washington. "Our early defeats, that freezing, starving winter at Valley Forge—they made soldiers of Americans. We begin to give the enemy fighting as hot as he brings us, and

111

hotter. But if the British are on their defense here, they threaten to attack us at the South."

He took up another paper and studied it.

"General Clinton sailed lately, with shiploads of troops, to attack Charleston and march through the Carolinas. We need brave men and good officers in those parts to face and fight him. You, Major, will leave your regiment here and go home to Virginia. Stir the people, raise us a force of stout mounted men, and lead it against the British. That is what I urge you, as a tried and seasoned patriot—"

He broke off and looked sharply at Nick.

"Ah, your face is long and troubled," said Washington. "I trust there is no ill news from your lady and your family."

"Nay, I heard by today's post that Mistress Nancy is well, and the younger children also," said Nick. "And our oldest son writes that he hopes to be worth his new lieutenancy with his rifle regiment. But the same mail brought word that an old friend—one you, too, will remember—is dead."

"What old friend, Nick?"

"I speak of Janus. You remember how he raced, and how later he shone as the sire of other racers." Nick still looked gloomy. "His age was thirty-four, ripe years for a horse. Colonel Jepthah Atherton in North Carolina owned him and sold him for a hundred and fifty pounds to John Goode."

"John Goode," Washington repeated the name. "Aye, he's of Mecklenburg County in Virginia, and a sound patriot."

"Janus was on his way thither, but the way was long and chilly for his aged bones. He reached the home of Herbert Haynes, between Atherton's and Goode's, and there he died. Haynes wrote to me, knowing I'd wish to be told."

Nick paused, and grimaced apologetically.

"You think it strange, General, that I mourn for an old horse. Yet he and I were friends and comrades, and I have gloried in him his life long. By thoroughbred mares he got sons and daughters who won at the heroic distance, and by others—Chickasaw mares, mostly, of Indian breeding—he became sire of many quarter horses. We won't look on his like again."

"Nay, I don't think your mourning is any whit strange," protested

Washington. "I say outright, Janus was a true four-footed American, brave and strong and useful."

Nick nodded.

"I should have thought in your manner, General," he admitted. "Janus lives on in his children. I myself have two Janus horses in my own stables at home. Others of his blood are to be found in all parts of the country."

"Janus has died, and so must all living creatures," went on Washington. "But his life and its end are good omens for America. Americans can father new bravery and strength to follow the old. America can prevail against heavy odds and win to greatness."

"Aye, sir, America must do just that," said Nick.

"And we must help America." Washington picked up the papers again. "If the war rises anew at the South, that is where the war must end."

"Victoriously," added Nick.

"Victoriously," Washington said after him. "Now, your attention on this matter of your part in the coming southern campaign."

Acknowledgments and Sources

A historical novel is fiction, written with close attention to known facts of the past. This book tries to retain what is known of the very real Janus, a horse of horses in colonial Virginia and ancestor of many splendid racers of the present day.

Among principal characters in the story, Nick Forrest, Nancy Tyll, Captain Magworth, Carr Thane, and the Booth servants Saul and Scipio are fictitious, though, it is hoped, convincing and accurate as the sort of people in the time and place. But Janus himself, Mordecai Booth and his wife and son, Booth's peppery mother-in-law Anna Armistead, William Byrd III, George Washington, and some minor characters are out of actual colonial history, as true to their real selves as it is possible to make them.

The research and its interpretation could never have been possible without the cordially competent help of the staff of Colonial Williamsburg. Books and papers from the archives, studies of what the town and region were like, permission to examine the splendid collections of colonial costumes and household furnishings, and a variety of verbal and written pointers by men and women competent to give them—all these helped. Special thanks is due to Mrs. Gay Holland of Durham, North Carolina, who excels both in riding horses and writing about them, for reading the manuscript in early stages and offering good advice about horses.

The *Virginia Gazette* might tell us much about Janus in 1756 and 1757, if files for those years could be found. Reliance must be on later reports of Janus and his contemporaries, notably John Hervey, *Racing in America, 1665–1865* (New York, 1941), I; Peter Cottom, ed., *The Gentleman's New Pocket Farrier* (Richmond, 1830); and Patrick Nisbet Edgar, *The American Turf Register, Sportsman's Record and General Stud Book* (New York, 1833). For general information, Jane Carson, *Colonial Virginians at Play* (Williamsburg, 1965), and various volumes of *Virginia Magazine of History and Biography* have been especially and rewardingly consulted.

Here are some references to the truth about Janus, arranged by Chapters:

I. Edgar (39) says Janus was imported from England "about the year 1752," which date is accepted by some historians. But Hervey, who did tireless research on his subject in America and abroad, says (I, 71) that Booth bought him from George Grisewood in 1756, which I have accepted. Janus is described by Hervey (I, 72).

II. George Washington was at Williamsburg in the summer of 1756. See Douglas Southall Freeman, *Young Washington,* Vol. II of *George Washington: A Biography* (New York, 1948), 198. Booth's near loss of Belleville to settle his debts, with its purchase by his mother-in-law and her disposal of it, is told in *Virginia Magazine,* LX (1952), 73 ff.

III. Emmie Ferguson Farrar, *Old Virginia Houses: The Mobjack Bay Country* (New York, 1955), 78–82, includes the history of Belleville, with several pictures and some facts about the Booths. Methods of treating Janus' lame shoulder are gleaned from Cottom, which has much on early veterinary medicine. The 1752 race at Gloucester, when Tasker's Selima beat the best horses in Virginia, is one of the few documented races of the time. It is described in the *Maryland Gazette,* Dec. 21, 1752, and is evaluated in Carson, 124. A portrait of Tayloe is in *Virginia Magazine,* XXXV (1927), facing 345.

IV. Janus' training toward new health and speed is based on the English methods of Arthur Taylor, as described in Cottom, 366–67. Taylor came to America with these methods before the end of the eighteenth century and was considered the foremost trainer of his time. Byrd's reckless gambling is noted in Carson, 51 ff. His portrait is in *Virginia Magazine,* XXXVI (1929), facing 242.

V–VI. The Christmas dance at Belleville is imaginary, with details borrowed from many accounts of such festivities. William Nelson was a prominent figure in the society of the time, and his young son Thomas became governor of Virginia. Lewis Burwell, too, is real. Details of the matching of Janus and Valiant at this time are imaginary.

VIII. As has been noted, known facts of the race are few. The letter of Elizabeth Hill Carter Byrd to William Byrd III of May 13, 1757, in *Virginia Magazine,* XXXVII (1929), 242–43, seems to be the only contemporary notice. Her mention of the "Race, that Mr. Page and Mr. Lewis made with Mr. Boothe" has suggested to some that it was a race of four horses, entered by Booth, Byrd, Page and Lewis. But Hervey (I, 72) calls it a match race of two only. Mrs. Byrd's language must have meant that Page and Lewis substituted for the absent Byrd as Valiant's sponsors.

Probably she meant Robert Page of Broadneck, a neighbor of Byrd. *Virginia Magazine,* XXXIV (1926), 275, says he died in 1768, at the age of forty-six, which would make him thirty-five at the time of the race. It is impossible to identify Lewis, and here he is fictionized as a gentleman rider. Carr Thane, too, is fictional. Although professional jockeys had ridden races in England since the late seventeenth century, Virginia owners usually rode their own entries. This choosing of fine riders for Janus and Valiant would be unusual for the 1750's.

IX–X. Here, too, the story is fiction, using the few known facts. The research staff of Colonial Williamsburg has located the old Williamsburg race track north of the present Chesapeake and Ohio Railroad tracks and east of U.S. Highway 60, at the northeast quarter of town. The ground is now occupied by homes and business enterprises. The track was in use by 1737, when races were advertised in the *Virginia Gazette,* July 1 of that year. J. F. D. Smyth, *A Tour in the United States of America* (London, 1784), I, 20, says that in 1772 the track was "a very excellent course." A manuscript of 1767, in the archives at Colonial Williamsburg, has some description, including the three poles that marked the starting point and judges' stand. Certainly it was one of the oldest and finest race tracks in colonial America and continued in importance until the eve of the War of Independence. See Carson, 257–59. Freeman (243) says Washington was in Williamsburg in late April, 1757. Surely his high interest in horses and racing would have brought him to watch Janus train.

XII–XIII. Mrs. Byrd's letter of May 13, 1757, tells her husband: "Your horse Valient lost the race" and leaves us to imagine how it happened. Details here were written after much study of various early matched races and with vivid memories of modern races.

XIV. This imaginary conversation takes place at Washington's New Jersey headquarters in early 1780. Janus' later career is summarized in Hervey, I, 72–73, and in Nelson C. Nye, *The Complete Book of the Quarter Horse* (New York, 1964), 18–19. Nye's long lists of quarter-horse champions and their pedigrees reveal that the Janus blood is widespread and triumphant to this very day.